THE FIRST TRUE LIE

THE FIRST TRUE LIE

MARINA MANDER

Translated from the Italian
by Stephen Twilley

CANONGATE
Edinburgh · London

Published in Great Britain in 2014 by Canongate Books Ltd,
14 High Street, Edinburgh EH1 1TE

www.canongate.tv

1

Originally published in 2011 in Italy as *La prima vera bugia* by et al S.r.l. Milan

This book has been selected to receive financial assistance from English PEN's 'PEN Translates!' programme, supported by Arts Council England. English PEN exists to promote literature and our understanding of it, to uphold writers' freedoms around the world, to campaign against the persecution and imprisonment of writers for stating their views, and to promote the friendly co-operation of writers and the free exchange of ideas.
www.englishpen.org

British Library Cataloguing-in-Publication Data
A catalogue record for this book is available on request from the British Library

ISBN 978 0 85786 549 6

Typeset in Van Dijck by Palimpsest Book Production Ltd, Falkirk Stirlingshire

Printed and bound in Great Britain by Clays Ltd, St Ives plc

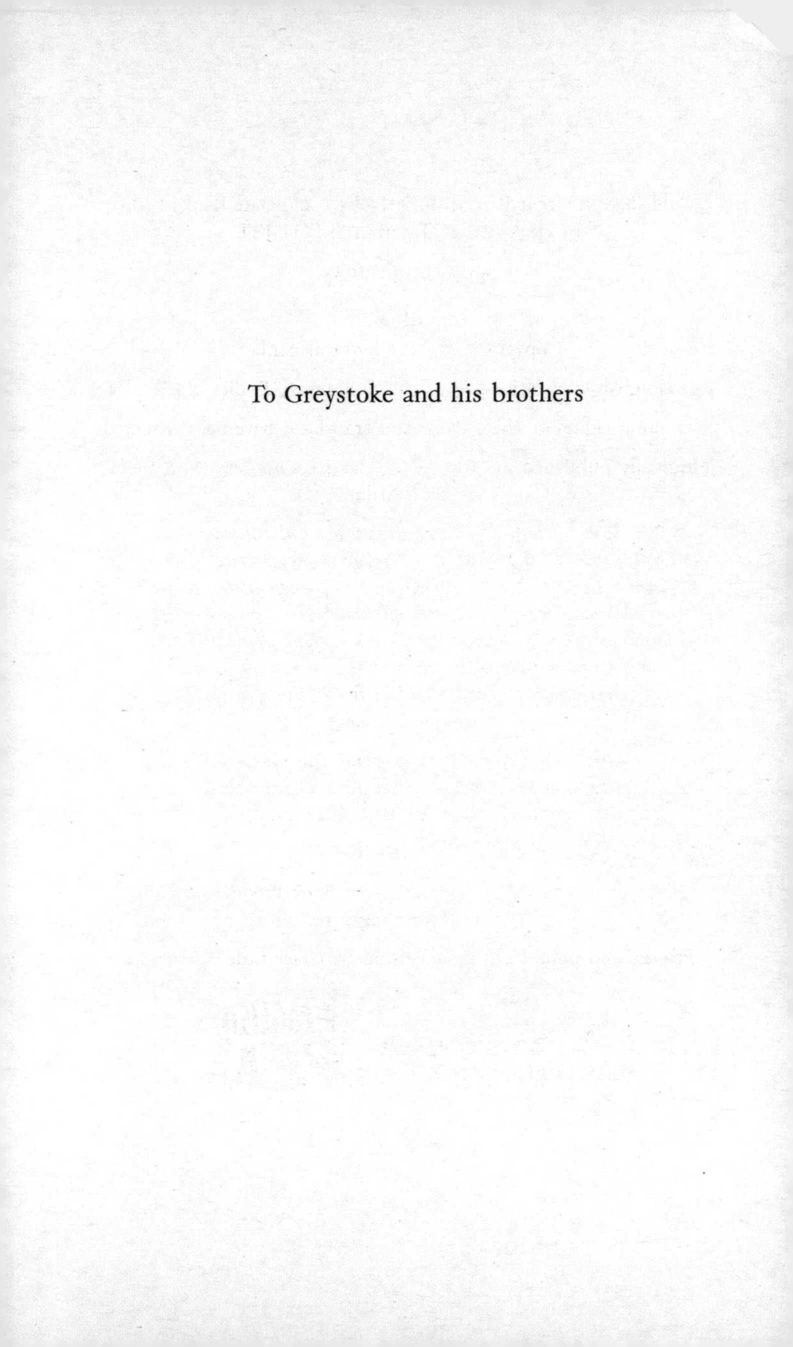

To Greystoke and his brothers

Some Days

Some days I wonder: What does it mean to be a half-orphan?

You can't know because you're a grown-up.

You've got parents who already seem like grandparents, a house where you're free to go into all the rooms, a car to get away in . . . There are so many things you can forget.

Mama's always saying 'I remember', but I'm not so sure about that, because sometimes it seems she really doesn't remember anything about what it's like to be my age. This happens a lot with adults.

The worst are the ones who take your toys and then don't even know how to play. They want to win, fine, but they can't handle losing, and as soon as you start to have fun they suddenly remember they've got an appointment, or they've parked the car badly, or else it's their kid.

'Sorry, love, but I really must be off now.'

Even worse are the ones who ignore you and shut themselves up in the bedroom with Mama.

'We're going to go in there for a bit and chat.'

They say they have to talk, but I know perfectly well they're having sex. They turn the lock so so slowly and hardly talk at all and every once in a while Mama mews and goes shhhh.

Mama thinks I never notice anything because her room is at the end of the hall, but I've realised if I want to protect myself I can't get distracted. I activate my periaudio, which is like a periscope but for the ears, and I try to pick out details. A periaudio isn't really an instrument, it's a sort of special attitude that makes it seem natural to notice more. They say for a child I'm extremely sensitive – whether they mean it as a compliment, I don't know. They say it with a smile, but there's something sad behind that nice smile that makes me think they haven't understood much of anything. I train myself to be sensitive, and my antennae tune in on their own.

I've learned that details say more than things do. If you pay attention to details you can convince adults that everything's fine. If none of your details are wrong they believe you.

Some examples of details that are wrong are: messy hair, mucky notebooks, dog-eared books, scratches, black fingernails, dirty words. Adults are obsessed with dirty words. Usually the words adults consider dirty aren't the ones I do.

'Stop swearing.'

'They're not dirty words, it's just things are like that!'

Take 'arseface': if someone has a face that looks like an arse, with a big, ugly crack sandwiched between cheeks like a stupid baby's bottom, it's not my fault.

I also get some satisfaction from 'fucking shit', even more than from the other *fuck* words that adults like: fucking hell, fuckwit, fuck off, and so on. Fucking shit really means fuck and shit together, it's like saying 'yuck' times two, like with the dog poos you find on the pavement. The ones our neighbour's dog does, for example, are huge. You're amazed and disgusted at the same time, just like with a fucking shit.

Saying *stronzetta*, which actually means 'little turd' but also 'snooty', is like sneezing, when your nose tickles and tickles. Stronzetta is more like Antonella, just to give you some idea. Antonella is beautiful, with long, straight, blond hair and dimples when she smiles – but she never smiles at you, as if you're nothing but a fucking shit. My grandma always used to pinch my cheeks to give me dimples.

'Come over here and let me give you some dimples like Cary Grant.'

'Leave me alone. I don't want dimples. Dimples are for babies.'

Running round the table, tripping over chair legs, hiding behind the waxed apples in the fruit bowl with different levels like a wedding cake.

'You'll never catch me, you old witch.'

'Don't talk to your grandma like that, you're nothing but a little brat.'

'Witchy witchy witch, what a fucking bitch.'

'Luca, who taught you to speak like that?'

There are certain words adults don't like and by now I've learned not to say them when they're around.

Adults like to use words like 'in-laws', 'power steering', 'holiday', 'colleague', 'mortgage', 'sciatica', 'nostalgia', and especially words that end in -gy like 'psychology', 'lethargy', 'strategy' and 'allergy'.

Mama, for example, suffers from all the '-gy's put together. She says that psychology's no use to her, that sleeping too much causes lethargy, that she's nostalgic for a man who's really a man, but that you still need a strategy to find him or else to make more money, that with the pollen every year her allergies just explode, and the vaccines aren't worth a damn.

As for me, I'm vaccinated against all this.

Mama complains constantly and sometimes it's

really kind of sad. But what's strange is that when she's truly sad she stops complaining. She just drifts around the house, super slow and without saying a word, like a pouty angel. The other day I got a quick look at her as I walked down the hall. Her bedroom door wasn't closed all the way. She was sitting on her bed and sniffling and her eyes were red and puffy, not because of allergies, I don't think.

It's not pretty seeing your mama cry, because you don't know how to help her, and also because you'd like to be the only one to cry in your house when you feel like it. You're not all that big yet, so even if it's not exactly fun you can still cry once in a while; you're allowed to because your friends still do it. I'm jealous of my classmates who can whine all day if they feel like it. I can't, because Mama's so sad and I can't be sadder than she is. We'd end up sinking. And we don't have a dad to save us, a fireman like after the terrorist attacks who takes you in his arms and carries you far away from danger, a dad like the dads in commercials. We're always a little bit in danger.

Mama says that Dad disappeared into the void. When she says it she looks up, over my shoulders, as if the void was still there, behind me, as if she was seeing a ghost. Naturally I turn round, but I don't see anything, just a painting with a choppy sea hung up over the sofa with the armrests all scratched up. A yucky painting full of yucky weather with a scribbly signature in the bottom corner.

'It's impressionist,' Mama explains, and it rather is.

I've never understood if Dad died for real, or if he only died for us the moment I came into the world. For all I know he could be having a good time on a motorcycle with some new mama, but I don't want to ask. It doesn't seem right to butt in. I make do with the official version. It's not as if it makes such a big difference, seeing as how he's not around. Usually I try to change the subject, like when Mama asks me about school and my classwork, and I concentrate on my index finger and find a little strip of skin to bite off, or else a little white spot on the nail, called a sweetheart, which is a sign of a lack of calcium, according to the doctor. And as a matter of fact Mama doesn't like me to drink lots of milk.

So let's say I've been an orphan, father-wise, more or less since the beginning – 'orphan' for that matter being the only word I hate and that adults hate too. With 'orphan' we're all in agreement.

Orphan in my case is like a coat with only one sleeve.

Kids use the word orphan like it's a dirty word.

Adults, on the other hand, when they say orphan they say it under their breath, like when they talk about diseases or disasters that fortunately happen to other people. There are loads of parents who decide to split up, loads of kids who see one or the other parent once in a while, but being an orphan, that's truly awful, like you're missing something and everyone only sees the part that's not there. You're not what you are – you're what you're missing. Like when someone has a glass eye. You look into the eye that doesn't see, not into the healthy one that's looking at you with all it's got. Anyway, being a half-orphan is a bit like a disease, because it makes you strange, and there are things you can't do without a father.

After Mama gave me my first bicycle she brought me to the car park to teach me how to ride. I pedalled my first three circles, trying not to hit the car bumpers or the bollards that looked like big *panettoni*, forcing myself to keep my balance even though I was so excited. On the third circle the front tyre went flat, going pssss, the sound of a butterfly fart, and Mama said, 'Ugh, who knows how to fix a flat tyre?'

And then I said, with the bike lying on the ground and my tail between my legs, 'It doesn't matter, let's go home.'

You get used to it though. I'm used to it now.

Of course, when Mama acts like that, when it seems like she doesn't have a clue how it feels to have to walk home with your new bicycle, I would do anything just to get her out of her doesn't-matter bubble, which she goes back into as soon as she can. She goes around with her nose in the air, as if she's not interested in anything. Or as if up there, on top of the houses, on top of everything, above the flat roofs and beneath the stomach-ache sky, where seagulls never fly, there's an answer, the solution we need, a puncture repairman, a sticking plaster shop closed for the holiday.

I feel like strangling her sometimes, I swear, but that's just an expression. I would never, ever want to become a complete orphan because then things get seriously messed up. If you're a complete orphan they take you and throw you in a home, they put a hand on your shoulder and walk you off to your cell. If you don't have a father, well, OK, but if you don't have either one, a mama or a dad I mean, they think it could be contagious, so they put you in a hospital where every-one's like you, even if they know perfectly well you can't get better. They shut you up in a kind of hospital and you have to follow orders. You don't have your own house any more, or your own room. All you've got is one fucking shit of an illness. That's also why I pay attention to details.

I remember seeing children like that in a film when I was little – lots and lots of children crammed into metal campbeds with rusty bed springs, like the ones in an orphanage, or in a prison or a mental hospital. People who are alone for whatever reason, it doesn't matter if they're old or young, they always end up in this kind of place, because no one knows where to put people who are alone, and so they stick them all together hoping they'll keep each other company.

I have to admit, every once in a while Mama does try to give me a new dad. But for some reason or other things never work out.

'One dad down, next one up.'

She says it like she's saying sorry. She shrugs her shoulders and sighs, then she pulls her neck back into her jumper, into the shell she carries around, and then she smiles with her eyes all bright and watery and hugs me in a way you can see is a big effort for her. It's as if lifting her arms is like lifting weights, and hugging me shifts a bit of that weight onto me. Mama thinks this joke is funny, but I know it's not her fault if it doesn't make us laugh.

Then she usually says, 'What do you say we go to bed? Tomorrow I have to get up early.'

The last dad, for example, he was nice enough, but I didn't like him because he had a scratchy beard and smelled like train seats. He seemed dirty. Actually, more than dirty, he seemed poor, and a poor dad's no good for us. If we really have to take one in he at least has to be normal and not embarrass us. I'm sick of being different.

At school they give us lots of speeches about how we have to accept all kinds of different people: immigrant kids, handicapped kids, down-and-out kids, the ones who don't eat prosciutto, or won't eat their meat rare, or only eat vegetables, the kids who don't eat at all, and the ones who stuff themselves every chance they get, who've got rolls of fat on their ankles and have trouble sitting cross-legged, like my friend Chubby Broccolo from Brindisi. I'm all for it, obviously. The fact is I wouldn't want a strange dad. On TV there are never dads with black hairs stuck in their face like nails, dads whose job it is to wash windshields at traffic lights, dads who even in the summer wear an anorak that's dirty round the collar – so why should we have to take one home with us? Mama agreed I was right about that, even if she's sad so much of the time. Mama is too pretty for someone like that. If he kisses her too much her face gets itchy.

'It's not a question of rich or poor, good-looking or ugly. Feelings are more complicated.'

Basically though, I know we think about it in the same way. The last few times they shut themselves up in her room to talk she wasn't mewing any more.

'How about if instead of a dad we get a dog?'

'I'm too tired for a dog.'

'But Mama, can't you see how great it'd be, a fucking big dog who takes fucking big shits?'

I said it like that because I was cross, but weirdly she didn't yell at me. Instead she actually smiled a little and raised her right eyebrow as if she was getting an idea.

'If you want, for your birthday, you can get a cat.'

So now we have Blue, who's like a cartoon cat. We called him Blue because of his breed and also because Mama loves the blues. Ah, the blues!

'Listen: the blues are like the sound of the sea; close your eyes and they'll rock you to sleep.'

Blue won't ever be a dog, but he's a great cat – he even likes Muddy Waters.

'Do you know why they called him that?' Mama asked me.

'Who?'

'Muddy Waters.'

'Dunno.'

'Because when he was a kid he used to play in the mud by the river and always came home covered in it.'

'Lucky him.'

Since we live on the eighth floor and don't have rivers and trees or other kinds of nature around us, Blue sharpens his claws on the yellow sofa. Every once in a while feathers come out of the cushions and he thinks they're little birds. If I throw Blue crumpled-up balls of paper he fetches them like a dog. He runs after them and ends up sliding across the floor, which drives him crazy, then he pretends nothing happened. But he puts the ball on your shoe, which is funny. It's only too bad I can't take him outside – if I put the lead on him he's out cold. The vet says it's narcolepsy, like the people who suddenly fall asleep because something happens to their brain, but it's nothing serious.

The vet is a nice guy. He's gentle and his eyes are big behind his glasses and he has a little tuft of white hair in the middle of his black fringe, like a badger. He loves animals. The sleeves on his shirts are too short and you can see long hairs coming out of them, hair that's fine and soft like a wolf pup's.

'Mama, what do you think of the vet?'

'What do you mean, the vet? Enough with your

nonsense. Do I have to change the cat's doctor along with my gynaecologist?'

I have to stop myself from going on or else Mama gets annoyed. When we leave the vet's smelling like fur and disinfectant, all three of us feel white and shiny, all healthy and beautiful. Last time a woman with a black and yellow fur coat like a leopard gave us really dirty looks. Her dog was dying. She glared at me for taking *A Kitten's Life* from the wobbly metal magazine tree that was filled with brochures about taking care of your puppy. It's not my fault if I've got a fantastic kitten instead of a dog that's dying, I'm sorry leopard-spot lady. I'm so sorry for you and especially for your dog and the leopards you wear.

Blue in his little carrier cage sticks his startled face between the bars. He's curious but also frightened by the tail lights and the noises of the road, hoping to be set free soon, if not in a meadow then at least at home. You shouldn't complain about your kitten's life, Blue. After all there are plenty who have it worse.

'But the vet is really talented, right?'

OK, OK, let's leave it, or Mama will get grumpy.

When Mama gets too grumpy wrinkles show up on her forehead, like the lines waves leave when they come and go on the sand all day. But when her bad mood is over it's fantastic. We play together, wrestling like men do and getting into tickle fights, or else we do tongue-twisters and I always win. With me the woodchuck chucks as much wood as it could, Peter Piper's peppers are perfectly pickled, and all the animals get on just fine, woodchucks, chickens, cows, iguanas and capybaras. I'm here, have no fear, no need to worry about anything. Mama and I laugh like crazy until it's late. The next day I hope it rains, or snows, or else a tsunami comes, as long as I don't have to get up. In the morning I think I'm on holiday and instead the alarm goes off – and keeps blaring on and on and on. What a rip-off.

When Mama has nightmares she says it's not even possible to sleep in peace in this world, and that's what I think too. Other times she says the pills have stolen her dreams, that sleep was just an inky black nothingness, and she wakes up confused and doesn't know which way is up. Sometimes she makes coffee without putting in the water, or else the coffee.

'Don't talk to me, don't ask me for anything. I don't know anything about anything this morning.'

When I get up I get up, but inside I stay horizontal. I'm walking upright but inside I'm still dreaming, snug as a bug in a rug, inside the second skin of my pyjamas. Even my pores are like a million closed eyes. I dream about an enormous hand that gently rubs me all over. I warm myself up all on my own, while my tingling legs begin to move, because obviously I'm running late.

'Hurry up.'

More words adults are always saying.

'C'mon, hurry up and get a move on. We're going to be late.'

They're the ones who ought to hurry. I've got all the time in the world, go and tell them that. Anyway, since I always get up and do everything that needs to be done, I know exactly how to do it by heart, just like the national anthem: '*Fratelli d'Italia, l'Italia s'è desta . . .*' I don't need anyone to tell me how the rest goes.

1

So today I make do on my own.

Never mind that Mama hasn't got up, I get up anyway. I get ready on my own.

It must be because of the pills for allergies, or for nostalgia, one or the other. Sometimes Mama overdoes it and sleeps more than usual. Or maybe it's narcolepsy, like what happens to the cat's brain. I should ask the vet about it.

She says that every so often the pills have strange effects, but she also says I shouldn't worry, that everything's OK.

'Sometimes I have trouble getting out of bed, but it's normal. With this cold weather who wants to be exposed, to the cold I mean, getting out from under the duvet?'

Anyway, I have to get moving, and to make sure my hair's not messy before I leave. I tiptoe out to the lift. I say hi to the man from upstairs.

'You're going to school on your own today?'

'Yes.'

The lift buttons pulse like my heart, which has started to beat faster. I don't know why.

'Yes, I do now, yes.'

I act proud. Maybe I really am proud to be doing things on my own. Or maybe I'm ashamed because I'd rather be getting in the shiny car of a shiny dad with all the dad accessories. But at the same time I'm ashamed to be ashamed because if Dad vanished into thin air – another one of Mama's expressions – it's not our fault. Maybe she's right: feelings are complicated, especially early in the morning. Maybe it's not important. So then I smile and get on my way. That way I don't mess up.

At school everything's normal. Everyone's ready to follow along with the lesson despite the pillow marks on our faces, the gunk in our eyes, the yawns we barely manage to swallow. The morning proceeds as usual, and as usual I pass the time inventing stories in my head. Then it's almost noon, and my stomach begins to grumble because it's annoyed and can't take any more. Fortunately it won't be long now. When I leave I pretend to be in a hurry. I ask a guy waiting out front for the time.

'Quarter past one.'

I smile politely. 'Are you waiting for someone?' I ask.

'Yes, my son, Giovanni. Do you know him? Perhaps he's in the same class as you.'

'No, we have some Matteos, some Davides, 'No, we have some Matteos, Some Davides, lots of Marias and even a Samantha with an "h", but no Giovanni.'

'Do you want a lift?'

'No, thank you. I really must be off now.'

Pretending to be in a hurry also gives the impression that you're important. If no one is waiting for you, what do you care about being in a hurry?

The flower woman pops out of her flower hut, which stands on the corner like a guardhouse. She's ugly and smells like flower stems that have been left in the water too long, in rusty metal vases like the ones on the grave of Mama's dad, my grandpa.

'My my, how impressive, walking home on your own now. You're quite the little man.'

Why doesn't she shut up? 'Little man' is another term I can't stand. Like I can't stand the flower woman.

'What have you got against the flower woman?' Mama would ask.

'She ate the goose.'

'You're still going on about the goose? C'mon, stop thinking about it.'

Mama and I won a duck at the fair by throwing coloured rings on bottlenecks that spin on a kind of merry-go-round. We kept it at home for a while, then the duck turned out to be a goose and Mama gave it to the flower woman so she'd keep it at her house in the country.

'The goose will be much better off in the open air, you'll see.'

The lift is broken, or else the old man has left the doors open and made it get stuck on the fifth floor, as he often does. Mama says he's got problems in his head. Sometimes she says, 'Poor man.'

Sometimes she says, 'Old fool.'

It depends what pops into her head. If she's carrying groceries or bottled water she usually says old fool.

I take the stairs: seven flights, two hundred and fifty-four stairs. I count them every time. Today I stop at one hundred and sixty-six. It doesn't make any sense to hurry if no one is waiting. Mama will still be in bed, dazed and sleepy. Or maybe she'll have come round. I start climbing again, taking the steps two at a time, the even numbers with the right foot. If I manage not to put a foot wrong Mama will be fine for sure. I hear Blue miaowing behind the door. He always does that when he hears me coming. He's happy I'm here.

Mama and Blue come towards me.

But Mama's not here. It's just Blue.

The apartment has a dark look to it. I walk straight down the seemingly endless hallway, hearing the dull thud of my steps on the carpet. After passing the row of framed drawings on the wall, old boats floating in a sea of rippled paper, I go into Mama's room. Nothing's changed.

Everything is the same as this morning. No movement at all.

The room is wrapped in the grey-blue half-light of winter and worn curtains. Mama is wrapped in the covers. Has she changed position or was she already hunched up like that?

What should I do?

I adjust the covers for her. She's curled up in a ball as she sleeps. Maybe she's cold.

I ask her if she wants anything.

'Are you cold, Mama? It's really cold outside, you know.'

She doesn't answer.

'Please, Mama, answer me. Why don't you say anything?'

I try shaking her but she doesn't react.

I didn't expect her to. She seems completely lost

inside herself, inside a dream so deep and far away that she's not showing any sign of life. You never know though.

Maybe Mama is dead.

I've never seen a dead body, so I'm not sure what one looks like. Actually, I did see one once beside the motorway, but it was covered with a sheet, so I really only saw a sheet, and it didn't make much of an impression. All the cars slowed down to look, but there wasn't anything to see. Mama and I were going away for the weekend. So was everyone else probably. We indicated and re-joined the flow of traffic. Mama turned on the radio; the DJ was talking rubbish. We had the sun on our faces, a strong, cocky sun that didn't have anything to do with the dead body.

Now Mama is covered up too. The only part that's not is her face on the pillow. Her hair is messy. It looks like the hair of the woman in that famous painting that has something to do with spring, or maybe summer, but hers is like the branches of a tree that's grown upside down, like roots without the ground. What should I do? Maybe I should comb it. It's always better to have your hair tidy. What should I do? Should I wait a little longer, or ask for help right away? I can't ask for help. If Mama is dead I can't tell anyone. If I tell they'll take me to the orphanage.

This is terrible.

I don't want to go.

I don't want to be a complete orphan.

Anything else would be better.

Better to say that Mama's left.

Or else say nothing, and act like it doesn't matter.

Better to find a way to make do. It can't be that difficult. Better to try and survive.

Better to keep it a secret and smile.

Better to use my imagination, to make myself come up with something special.

Better to hope it will all just be over soon.

Better to do three thousand press-ups in a row, seven flights of stairs on one leg, long division in my head.

Better to bury Kolly the koala.

Better to think about what's better.

Better to believe that in a little bit Mama will be much better.

Is it true, Mama, in a little bit you'll be better?

But if Mama's dead, what could be worse?

I have to pay attention to details and remember not to cry. If I start crying I'll say that a gnat flew into my eye – or no, I'll say it was a stag beetle. That way they'll think it's a joke and won't make a big deal about it – or else a stag deer, same thing.

We're sitting on the bed, Blue and I, and we don't know how to act.

Blue trots back and forth and pokes his head here and there, wrinkling his nose as if he's hunting for something. He steps on the faded flowers of the bedspread, sniffs Mama, scratches with his paw and makes a little hollow in the sheet. He gets a claw stuck and looks at me with wide-open eyes.

'I don't know what to tell you, Blue, I'm sorry. There's nothing I can do about it.'

Suddenly a gigantic nothing starts to swirl and grow in my brain. My brain is a blank notebook that's never been opened, with nothing written in it, and no stories come into my head. There aren't even lines where I can hang any words I come up with. The nothing that's flooding my head and fogging my vision won't let me do anything. A huge expanse of nothing, like ice – Father Christmas has passed by, but the snow has wiped out his tracks. Blue has soft little pads on the bottoms of his paws. He doesn't leave any tracks. The reindeer have disappeared. There are some mounds in the distance, maybe they're igloos, ice-cube houses. I feel really cold. I'm afraid of houses made of ice cubes.

Father Christmas doesn't exist; I've known that for a while. There's a white stuffed toy, a polar bear drifting on his iceberg, who doesn't know whether he'll reach his destination or not. You see the image everywhere.

I feel stuffed myself.

Doctor Foster went to Gloucester, in a shower of rain. He stepped in a puddle and now we're all in fucking shit.

I can't call the doctor.

Time passes, I don't know how much.

On autopilot I find myself back in the living room. Blue and I squeeze up together on the sofa. Under his fur Blue is teeny-tiny. I go into my room. Blue follows me. I throw myself on the bed. I get up, go back to where I was before. I look in Mama's dictionary for what it says under the word 'Death', if there are details, more detailed details, something to make me understand what's happening. The dictionary is so heavy it's hard to pick up.

It says: 'The end of the life of a man, animal, or plant.'

That's what it says, and then a hyphen: 'accidental, sudden, slow, immature', then a semicolon, etc., etc. That is to say it says nothing. It's not true that you can find answers in books.

And then to drop dead, to die a sudden death, dead tired, extremely tired, OK. OK, I'm dead tired too but

I don't believe I'm dead. In books people never die for real, and not in the movies either.

I let the dictionary fall to the ground. It drops dead too, its pages thrown open at the letter 'D' like a cowboy shot down by Indians: you've got me, you devils. We go into the kitchen. Blue circles me like the stupid ballerina in Grandma's music box. He seems fake too. His stiff whiskers are like her lace tutu. I put a pizza in the microwave. In a few minutes the pizza in the microwave heats up and comes back to life. I burn my tongue on the mozzarella and the tip goes numb. I stick it out to show Blue but he's not interested. He's also numb, and only wants a piece of pizza. Eating and sleeping – that's all Blue is interested in. I'll do what he does, even if I also have to go to school and do homework. If Mama is dead I'll even have to do the grocery shopping, to bring home food for the family. I look for her purse to see if we have a little money to get by. We have a lot, actually, so at least there's that. There's also her bank card; I'll have to find the secret code. I'll have to practise with money, because I'm not very good at it. I get confused by all the zeros, which seem like bubbles, impossible to hold onto. There's also her mobile phone. I turn it off. Mama doesn't like me rummaging in her bag, but I don't have a choice.

If she doesn't hurry and wake up, I just . . . I don't know.

If she saw me she'd yell at me, but she doesn't see me, doesn't think about me, doesn't want me. She couldn't care less what it means to be an orphan at my age. She's got her own problems, things I wouldn't understand. Her problems are bigger because she's bigger. I'm only a child, or an only child; it's the same thing, just depends how it comes out. Sunset over the Black Sea or the Red Sea at Night, depending on how you look at the painting.

I don't know what she sees.

Adults can go away if they want – not me. I don't have anywhere else to go. I'm stuck here with her and her endless sleep at the end of the hall. I activate my periaudio but I don't hear a thing; it's as quiet as a grave. A periaudio is how bats hear when they're finding their way in the dark. It's a system for not smashing your face into obstacles, or at least for not doing it too hard, but this time I can't get it to work. I've got to stay with her even though she's stopped talking to me and listening to me. I've got to look after the cat, who's always hungry, and look after myself too.

Mama is a bitch. A bitch and an arsehole. All adults are bitches and arseholes. Bastards. Stinkers. Shitheads.

Idiots. Retards. Stupid arseholes. Shitty stinking arseholes. Pricks. Morons. I hate them.

It's like hate in dreams, where if you hate something you really hate it, and if you like something you really like it, like whole ocean liners full of hot chocolate and whole afternoons with Antonella, or else having Arseface tossing piles of fucking shit in your face. When I can't do anything, I hate, *hate* not being able to do anything. But what can I do?

Please, Mama, I'm begging you to tell me what to do.

I feel like crying. I don't know if it's right to cry, but I think it's normal in situations like this. A normal child would cry, and so I cry as much as I can. No one can see me anyway. Hot water gushes from my eyes while the polar bear on his cold slab is carried away by the current.

When all of my tears run dry I turn on the TV.

'Sometimes stupid programmes help me not to think.'

Let's hope Mama is right.

On TV a famous chef is giving cooking lessons. He beats eggs in front of a group of women wearing evening gowns who copy everything he does, batting their eyelashes and clattering their bracelets against the pots. I could make a cake for Mama, for when she wakes up.

For teatime, she says, because that's what Grandma used to say. But a cake's too complicated. Instead I'll make baked apples for her; it's not hard.

All the recipe needs is apples, sugar to taste, water and lemon rind.

They're good to have when you feel bad. Even if the smell smells like the hospital.

I've only been in the hospital once, when I had bronchopneumonia. The nurses – old hags with scuffed shoes – came in the night and replaced my biscuits with apples. Mama couldn't believe that nurses would steal a kid's biscuits.

I cut the apples in four and sprinkle sugar over them. The apples float in the pot like icebergs, like sinking ships to taste, like the *Titanic*. When they're ready I pour them into a bowl, wait for them to cool a bit, and then carry them in to Mama. I try not to trip on the carpet in the hall. The bowl clinks against the plate as though my hands are shaking.

I leave the bowl on her bedside table because Mama doesn't want baked apples right now.

A book called *Enduring Love* lands on the floor with a thud. Mama doesn't notice. On the cover is a picture of a hot-air balloon with people in it, rising into the sky.

The phone rings. Mama doesn't hear it.

The phone is sitting on the ground and the cord is all twisted.

'Mama went out. Yes, later. Bye.'

I cross my fingers because I'm telling a lie.

'It was Giulia, Mama. Don't you want to talk to Giulia?'

Giulia is Mama's friend, the one she spends hours with, complaining about everything. Giulia complains about everything but she's happier. It seems like she only does it to keep Mama company. They talk about men a lot, usually not nice things.

'You don't have to tell me. Remember who you're talking to.'

A couple of Sundays ago we took a trip to the country with Giulia. Giulia's not bad even though she does have red fingernails, which I don't like.

'Look, you've got red fingernails like a chicken.'

She didn't get offended. She even laughed.

'That's because I *am* a chicken!'

There were chickens in the courtyard outside the restaurant where we went to eat.

'Don't touch the chickens. They're dirty. And wash your hands.'

There were also all colours of rabbits, so soft you wanted to pet them.

I'll never eat rabbit again, I swear, never again, and not horse and not even lamb.

'Not even *gelato*?'

'What's gelato got to do with it? Gelato doesn't have fur.'

Furry animals are my favourite. I want to have all kinds. In my opinion people who like animals are nicer, and they understand people better too. It'd be great to be a vet and take care of the big animals, lions and leopards and cheetahs – that's what I want to do when I grow up, be a vet for big cats. At home we've got a film about lions. We never get tired of watching it, Mama and I. She says she likes lions because they're strong and muscular, that when they roar they 'give us an idea of infinite power', that the lion's roar is the sound of the centre of the earth or of what we were before becoming domesticated.

She says she'll take me to see them, some day.

'When you're older, when we have more money.' When whatever.

Africans say God created cats so men could pet lions.

For now I watch the documentary. For now I've got nothing else to do.

Blue curls up near me and starts to purr.

I feel like there's too much silence in the house.

When there's too much silence it makes more noise than noise does, like the deaf kids I meet on the tram sometimes. They're going to the deaf school where they can understand each other with hand gestures, but on the way there they make a ton of crazy sounds and you don't have any choice but to listen. If one of them gets his ticket jammed in the machine he may as well have a fishbone stuck in his throat.

Silence, on the other hand, fills up your head like the blank notebook, and it's too big to do anything about it.

There's a time just before dinner, before the day ends, when you feel the silence more strongly. At most there are cars going by and quickly zooming away. They're inside the life that's outside, beyond our window, beyond the television screen; they're part of the noise of TV programmes, of things that happen far away. Then usually Mama gets home and starts messing about with dinner. Even if I'm in my room I can hear the noises coming from the kitchen, cupboards slamming, the mosquito buzz of the electric can opener, a metallic rummaging through the cutlery drawer. It's over, I tell myself, it's all over. We're safe. I go to her. I circle round her like a tsetse fly. Tsetse flies are torture for lions too. Lions sleep two thirds of the day and wake up in the evening to eat. Since it's winter it gets dark early; it's already pitch black at five.

Every two minutes I feel like going into her room to see if something's happened, if Mama has tasted the baked apples, but I'm afraid of finding out that she hasn't even touched them and being disappointed.

Better to wait for evening; in winter evening comes soon.

Patience is a virtue, fine, I get it. I've got all the time in the world.

Inside my eyes there's nothing but blackness. When I open them everything is dark.

I must have fallen asleep. I feel cold, the film's finished. Rain taps on the window, otherwise it's quiet. The shapes of the furniture are the backs of elephants in the savannah. The dark stain of the painting looms over my head.

Even Blue is snoring. Every so often he makes a sucking sound. Maybe he's dreaming about sucking milk, because in dreams milk doesn't give him the runs; salami doesn't cause spots, nostalgia, melancholy . . . The great thing about cats is that even when they grow up they stay kittens.

Blue always tries to get some milk when I have

breakfast, but I can't give it to him because milk upsets his tummy. Once he threw up on Mama's bed and she had to put everything in the washing machine.

'I swear I'll throw the cat in too.'

She wasn't being serious though, just joking.

I've got a nasty taste in my mouth, like I ate something rotten. Maybe I'm sick too, like Mama. And I won't wake up again. I cross the room like a sleepwalker, shuffling with my arms out in front of me as I look for the light switch. I turn on all the lights. I turn the TV back on. I turn everything on, the stereo and the radio too; that way the house seems full of people.

I go into Mama's room: she's still turned off.

I look for a detail telling me she's moved. I don't know . . . maybe her hair. I don't think so. I wonder if she was exactly like this before. I call her name, shout at her, pinch her. Nothing. I feel my face getting wet again, feel like I can't swallow, feel my legs wobble, and my chin and my voice, I feel something hot in my stomach. She doesn't feel anything any more. I think she really is dead.

I curl up next to her. The pillow gets flooded. I stay like this until I realise it's not possible to stay like this for ever.

When I go into the bathroom my eyes are red, my

face looks like I've got the flu. I pick up the toothpaste and squirt some in my mouth, without the toothbrush, to get rid of the disgusting taste that's all over my tongue. I feel sick, like I've just done a hundred thousand corners in the car, hurtling down a roller-coaster.

I'm still cold. Maybe I've got a temperature. In the other room everyone's shouting: the guy on the news, the radio announcer, Jovanotti singing how it rains, how it pours. When Mama wants to see if I have a temperature she puts her lips to my forehead, but I can't do it to myself. Fucking shit. I take the thermometer from the medicine cabinet, shake it up and down, and put it under my arm. Then I change my mind – there's no point in having a fever now. I lean my forehead against the edge of the sink; it's nice and cool. I stay bent over for another two or three centuries, until my back starts to hurt like an old person's. Blue's standing in the doorway. He looks at me but doesn't understand. He tries to miaow but nothing comes out. Even he doesn't know what to say.

It was only a little while ago that I woke up, but I'm really tired. I should do my homework, but I don't know if I'm up to it. Someone whose mother's just died can't do homework, but that isn't an excuse, because I can't tell anyone about it. It has to stay a secret, a really big secret just between us. I don't want to end up in an orphanage.

When I was younger Mama used to read me a story about a little girl who was left in an orphanage. At night the girl would hide under the blankets, even though they scratched her face. She was sad because nobody loved her. Then she was saved by a friendly giant who only ate snozzcumbers. He came through the window and carried her away. She stopped being just one orphan in a thousand and became the daughter of a big, strong man. But I stopped believing in giants – whether I liked it or lumped it, as Mama would say – a long time ago.

I have to do my homework. I can't risk them suspecting anything.

There was one boy at school who told a story about how he hadn't done his homework because his aunt had died – then they discovered it wasn't true at all and made him go to a million meetings to figure out how he'd ended up telling such a *whopper*. He earned an Unsatisfactory for behaviour. His aunt was pretty upset about it, especially because she wasn't decrepit at all.

The telephone rings again. I run to turn off the noise. It's Giulia again.

'My mother said she'll call you tomorrow, she's cooking.'

'No worries, I'm leaving, going on holiday, God willing. I'm already at the airport. I'll be back in a few weeks. Say goodbye to your mother and give her a kiss for me, and be good.'

'I will. Send us a postcard.'

Giulia says goodbye in a voice that's so happy it's gross. She doesn't notice anything. She's got other stuff on her mind.

Eating is gross. I don't think I'll ever eat again. I don't know what to do. It's my first dinner without a good dinner, my first night without a good night. For the first time in so long, maybe ever. I'll have to get used to doing without Mama. When she grazes my cheek it seems less like a kiss than a warmish breath of air, bringing me luck. I decide to sleep on the sofa. So long to my room, to the toys scattered across the floor, to the bears on the shelf secretly looking and laughing at me.

'You're nothing but a race of stupid, weak bipeds.'

So long to all the things I'm leaving behind.

The only one I take is the koala.

'What do you think?'

Kolly doesn't answer. He must be offended, because ever since I got Blue I've stopped asking for his opinion.

Old Kolly is made from real koala fur, with a brown

nose that's always cold. Someone Grandma knew in Australia sent it to me.

'I was very fond of this friend, you know. He was tremendously handsome when he was young, and an amazing dancer as well, but then he went away and I haven't seen him since.'

At that point Grandma's already off on a tangent that's filling her mouth with the words 'fond', 'friend', 'Australia' . . . Australia like Asturias or Austria-Hungary, obscure places on a map that went out of date a hundred wars ago, the Australia of, 'My dear, dear boy, it's on the other side of the world. When it's dark here the sun's up there; when it's winter here it's summer there.'

The Australia of kangaroos and duck-billed platypuses.

And then Mama, who never wants to go away anywhere, says with a swoosh of a voice that seems like a wingbeat: 'And birds of paradise, can you imagine? It must be paradise on earth. Maybe we should all go off to Australia, every last one of us.'

Who knows if Kolly would like to go back to his part of the world and climb the eucalyptus trees.

'What do you say, Kolly? Would you like to go and visit your relatives on the other side of the world?'

* * *

We could also go and sleep with Mama, but if she's really dead I'm not sure I want to be close to her. If she's dead she's already an angel. She'll come and visit me without me even hearing her steps on the wooden floor, without running into the furniture, without hurting herself on the corners. She'll come in her silk nightgown and, like a guardian angel, she'll make it so I dream in colour. She'll move like a rapper, gliding along without touching the ground. I don't even know any more if guardian angels exist. They'll tell you so many whoppers with the excuse that you like stories, but you're never completely sure if they're true or not. Or maybe Mama will transform into a zombie. I feel like a zombie myself now, but Mama is too beautiful to become a monster. She's never a monster, even when she gets mad and makes a nasty face. Eventually it passes and she goes back to being nice. She's nice now too, it's just that she forgot to wake up.

Grown-ups forget so much. Especially among themselves. They'll see each other for a while, they'll call each other, they'll chat, say 'my dear', 'my darling', and then forget each other.

'Sometimes people just fall into oblivion.'

Oblivion is like a long hallway, but vertical, a hole like the one on the landing we throw rubbish down, with scratchy cement walls and a shiny grey hatch like a sulky mouth. People fall into the hole, plop, and then stay there, squashed one on top of the other, waiting until someone wonders what ever happened to them.

'For example, do you remember that one guy, what was his name? Who knows what ever happened to him?'

That one guy, like my father, or maybe it is my father.

I think Mama and I have fallen into someone's oblivion too, because people don't seek us out so much, maybe because she's sad and when she's sad she's not much fun. You've really got to love her to put up with her then. Only if it's your own mother can you be OK with it – you can't do anything else; she's the only one you've got.

We've definitely fallen down the memory holes of the dads, my real dad's and those of the other ones as well, the contenders. Now it really seems like everyone has forgotten everything, that the world is far, far away, like in science-fiction films when you see Earth from another planet.

I'm sure there's lots of life on other planets, it's just that we're light years away here in the mega-galaxy of the eighth floor. There are lights in the windows across the street, people carrying dishes from the dining room to the kitchen, TVs that flicker with a bluish light, but we've lost touch, even Mama says so.

'You know how it is, in this city it's so easy to lose touch.'

It would take a super remote controller to beam yourself into those living rooms where big families eat popcorn in front of a good film, where they celebrate proper Christmases with great big Christmas trees that touch the ceiling with their golden tips.

I hate Christmas because none of this ever happens. I hate the candied fruit in the panettone, I hate the crooked figurines in the nativity scene in the school lobby, and the fat priest with the sticky hands who wants to bless me.

'Go with God, my son.'

'No thanks, if you're coming too.'

It always turns out that I get sadder because I'm supposed to be happier. I can't wait for Christmas to be over so I don't have to think about it any more.

There are presents, of course, but they're not always enough.

'Aren't you going to unwrap your gifts? That one with the red bow is from me; the lilac-coloured one is from Grandma; that one with the aeroplane paper is from Giulia. Happy Christmas, my pet.'

Already the day after Christmas is better.

And tomorrow will already be better too. Maybe tomorrow things will be different, my pet. All I have to do is make tomorrow come soon.

I bring the duvet with the clouds onto the sofa, along with Blue and the koala. The alarm clock quietly beams green Martian codes my way. I try to close my eyes.

It's strange to sleep with the light on, but I don't feel like turning it off tonight – it's better this way. On the inside of my eyelids I see swarms of microbes crazily moving about, like when you look into a microscope and spot the ones responsible for who knows what disease, or when you stare at a clear sky, when it's really, really clear, that's inhabited only by millions of quotation marks without words, without explanations, without motives.

At Grandma's house, where it's dark even during the day, when the sun comes through the shutters, the dust particles dance in the air, glittering like metallic paint. A ray of cosmic dust penetrating the lazy half-light of the afternoon, a sword that shimmers with all the colours of the rainbow and grants special powers, makes me a secret knight of the great disorder's higher order, a master cherry-stone spitter.

Deep in the darkness there was also the music room, with its armchairs covered in ghost sheets, the coat rack covered in ghosts' overcoats, and the forgotten instruments no one used any more but absolutely no one was allowed to touch.

'Practise on this', Grandma would say, handing me a mandolin for slicing the hard-boiled eggs.

The piano was opened only for my grandfather's funeral. Grandma sat down on the upholstered stool, stiffly erect, her eyes bright from crying or from too many toasts in her husband's honour: 'A good man after all.'

She began to play military marches, bobbing her purple hair from side to side, maybe in celebration of finally having become the supreme commander of the whole shebang. My grandmother has purple hair, a detail that has always really made me laugh.

2

I hear an ambulance siren, coming closer and closer. It's here. It's parked in the living room or under the bed. It's deafening me. I stick my fingers in my ears but it's no use, the noise continues. I wake up in a sweat. The alarm clock bores into my sleep like the drill they use to break up the street down below. I fling a heavy arm out of bed to turn it off. It was only a bad dream. Everything's all right. Then I remember. Nothing's all right. Not one single thing. What am I doing here on the sofa?

Mama didn't get up this morning either.

There's too much silence now I've turned off the siren and the demolition hammer that was hollowing out my head.

Mama's not getting up any more.

Now I remember everything.

I sit up and contemplate the new situation: the panorama of the furniture in the living room, a room both familiar and strange at the same time, like being in a hotel or someone else's house. Blue gets his purr-motor running.

I have to find some courage.

I don't have any courage.

I'm in a daze, sitting on the sofa with my legs and arms open wide, waiting for another pair of arms to pick me up, to pose me like she used to for baby pictures, a naked, confused newborn in the middle of the bed, like the picture of Grandpa when he was little, a chubby little grandfather dressed up in frills, looking nothing like the bony old man I knew.

I tell my feet to shake off this sluggishness, tell my legs to carry me down the hall to see how things are going, tell my head to be a bit more optimistic. But they're not the least bit interested.

At times like these it's usually Mama who comes to get me moving.

Now I have to get myself moving. I tell myself I have to get used to it: 'You've got to get used to it. You've got to manage. You can't be afraid of going down the hall.'

I argue with myself out loud.

'Mama's never frightened you before; she can't frighten you now. Can't you see she can't even move?'

As a matter of fact, she is still still.

Extremely still.

Nothing to be done.

There's only one hope – that she'll be resurrected, like Jesus. After three days. We've just begun the second, and who knows if it's true that Jesus was resurrected. They say he was, but I don't know if I believe it. Even Grandpa didn't really believe it was possible to go in and rise back out of graves, and anyway when he died he wasn't resurrected; he just died and that was that. He wanted a glass of wine on his grave instead of flowers. Mama said it was because he'd been in the war and seen so many dead people, that he stopped believing in God and in all those religious stories, because in this world there is no religion. In fact looking at all the people who die for no reason – I'm not just talking about bad people but good ones too – it's hard to believe there's an invisible someone protecting us. I'm not particularly interested in these things, even if now I could really use a God or some such thing to give me a hand. If there was one this would really be the time to prove it.

He could tell me what to wear to school. It has to be a clean shirt because Mama would never send me to school with yesterday's shirt – actually, he could wake up Mama, if he can. I can't. But God probably has more important things to do.

I have to wash as well. If I was sure Mama was back today I wouldn't bother, but since I'm not I can't risk them noticing anything strange on account of details, like the ones that betray people in *Columbo*. Lieutenant Columbo always looks rumpled just so everyone will underestimate him. Obviously if he was the suspect he'd change his raincoat.

I put on a striped shirt; it'll do fine. And a green jumper. I wash my armpits but forget the bidet, who cares – it's not like anyone's going to be inspecting my underwear.

'If you don't wash below too you'll have moss and lichens growing there, like in the taiga and the tundra.'

Mama always exaggerates.

Blue licks himself to get clean. I'm so jealous. Blue has eighteen whiskers per side and long hairs like whiskers above his eyes. When I don't have anything else to do I count them, to see if there happen to be any more, since Blue is growing up too: no longer a kitten, as the flower woman would say, but becoming quite the little cat.

'OK, Blue, time for din-dins.'

'Din-dins' is Blue's favourite word. If you say it to him he gets all excited and begins to follow you around and won't stop until you give him something. Blue jumps on the table, slips past the box of cereal, the sugar, the glass ashtray from Venice that's a bit chipped on one side, and launches himself at the can of mackerel pâté as if he hasn't seen food for I don't know how long. A bit later, in all his enthusiasm, he pushes his bowl under the sideboard and then looks at me in surprise, as if to say, 'Help! Where'd my din-dins go?'

Cats do things like that. They're really intelligent and sometimes stupid. They understand everything, but when it comes to food they know nothing.

Blue rubs himself, all soft and silky, against my legs. I'd like to have a sleeping-bag body like Blue and snuggle down inside myself and pull up the zip. I'd also like to have a tail and wag it when I'm cross, make it bristle when I meet arsefaces, and hold it straight up when I'm happy and feel like walking with my head high.

Maybe I'd like to be Blue. Who could go back to purring with Mama.

'Did you feed Blue?'

Usually, before going out, Mama asks me, 'Did you feed Blue?'

She only asks to nag me, because she knows very well whether I've done it or not. If I go back to show her the bowl she says, 'Hurry up.'

If I hurry she says, 'Get a move on.'

Before leaving I check up on Mama, but without going into her room. I look at her from afar. I'm in a rush.

I have to run. Whenever I do the corners of the books in my backpack poke my back. I've got to tighten the straps, or else leave the house sooner next time and then walk normally.

It's freezing cold; when I breathe I can see my breath. If I can see my breath it means I'm alive, even if I'm dying of cold.

It's the coldest winter since nineteen hundred and something, and it's windy too, which it almost never is. The wind helps with the pollution; it reduces the fine particles, the sneakiest ones, the ones that get in everywhere without anyone seeing them and then make you sick.

Fortunately we don't live far from school.

We're three thousand seven hundred steps away, more or less, because every time I count them the number is different.

I run into Davide at the entrance – just as well – we'll come in together.

Inside, along the corridor with all the drawings pinned up, there's a sign that says 'No Running'.

I ask Davide if he believes in God, and he replies, 'Are you stupid or what?'

And we rush to class.

I realise I've asked Davide a pretty odd question, out of the blue and so early in the morning. I've got to be careful not to let strange stuff like that slip out.

'Do you see this? It's a piece of granite that's become part of my hand. It's my rock-hand. Touch it.'

My desk-mate has scabs on his hands because yesterday he popped a wheelie on his skateboard and landed on the gravel. He picks at the clotted blood on his knuckle and gets blood on his exercise book. The blood doesn't stop. It spreads over the page and Mrs Squarzetti panics, fearing a haemorrhage.

'Oh my God, a haemorrhage!'

Rock-hand is taken downstairs to have his war wounds tended to. Later Rock-hand will sport a new plaster.

I like plasters a lot. I put them on even when I haven't hurt myself at all. Sometimes I'll draw on my skin a little bit to make it look more real. Plasters give the impression of an adventurous life, of someone who falls down but doesn't really hurt himself.

'What did you do to yourself?'

'It's nothing, just a little karate chop. I broke seven bricks with a single blow.'

'No way!'

The incident with my desk-mate is the most exciting event of the morning.

At the sight of blood Antonella grimaces as if she's going to pass out. I feel like throwing up because real blood turns my stomach, but I hold out; it's just the soul of the red biro gushing everywhere because yet again I've swallowed the cap. I think about my heavenly soul that may not even exist. I look at Antonella's heavenly blue eyes. She gets more beautiful every day and I blush just at the thought that she could be looking at me.

I hold out even though feeling sick makes me regurgitate a memory from nursery school: little spaghetti hoops floating like lifebelts in a pool of tomato sauce; a kid who's honking like an elephant and the next thing he's at the blackboard throwing up his cafeteria lunch, and it's making people laugh but also throw up themselves; the smell of vomit that stays in your nose even afterwards, even now. I hate pasta with tomato sauce. If there must be sauce at least let it be on the side, without everything mixed together. With things like that, if you meet with the school psychologist they'll tell your parents you've been traumatised, as if you've discovered you've only got one parent instead of two, or your Mama's sleeping with someone else's dad.

'Childhood trauma.'

It's just smaller when it comes to pasta with tomato sauce.

In any case I hold out. I don't want everyone to see what I've eaten for breakfast: a bowl of dry cereal exactly like Blue's cat biscuits. I swallow and it tastes like acid, and also like yoghurt, even though the yoghurt was already gone this morning. I licked the container and tried to reach the bottom with my tongue. I cleaned the tinfoil lid until all I tasted was tinfoil, the kind that shocks your back teeth.

Outside it's started raining again, and it's not the good rain any more, the impressive kind. It's a useless kind of rain, which makes you sleepy and the outlines of things fuzzy, and makes you think it will never stop.

It's raining like that inside me too.

Usually when I'm bored in class I read under my desk, or draw, or go over Mama's words in my head, trying to discover their secrets. 'Nostalgia': tender, burning desire for people, places and things she'd like to return to. 'Sciatica': extreme pain in the sciatic nerve that doesn't let you go skiing. And so on. I invent private exercises, count the holes the woodworms have worm-eaten out of the window frames over the centuries and centuries, amen, so the hours go by faster.

Sometimes I pay attention with one part of my brain and with the other I daydream. I imagine that past the roof and the chimneys and the TV aerials, there's the sea and the clear sky and ships with pirates. The pirates don't hunt whales any more; they hunt the people who hunt whales. The shitting pigeons on the windowsill are albatrosses perched on the ship's mainmast. I don't tell anyone I can do it because adults don't think it's so easy. They think you have to do one thing at a time; that you can't talk and eat, put on trousers and walk, draw and learn, dream and stay awake. If I think about something totally different I just have to pay attention where my eyes wander, otherwise it seems like I'm seeing ghosts, like Mama when she says that Dad vanished into thin air and she stares at the painting with the yucky weather.

At home, whenever I can't stand it any more, I close myself in the wardrobe that no one ever opens. I sit on top of the drawers in the middle of the clothes that smell like mothballs, and the herringbone overcoats and the cloth sacks I used to take to nursery school, blue-and-white checked with my name embroidered on them, still smelling like bread and chocolate. I stay there and think for a bit with the old overcoats on my face. I might cry if I really have to, and wipe my snot with the sleeve of an old shirt. Then I get over it, and then I don't want Mama to worry too much.

Mama. Mama. Mama.

The memory of Mama explodes again in my head.

A geyser of fear. I'm so afraid that someone will notice something.

'Do you know what the doctor said to the skeleton who showed up for an appointment?' I write on a piece of paper and pass it to Davide.

He shakes his head: No.

I write on another piece of paper, 'Couldn't you have come earlier?'

Out of the corner of my eye I can see him laugh.

I'm safe.

Everything's OK.

When we get out it's pouring.

Needles of freezing rain everywhere. I forgot to bring a hat. To stay out of it I'm forced to pass close to Arseface. It's a risk I have to take because I can't risk getting sick. I cross my heart and hope to die he doesn't say it again: 'Orphan-orphan-orphan', repeated like an evil chant.

Not too long ago, I'll never forget it, I was with my friends and Arseface said, 'Orphan-orphan-orphan.'

And I thought, Now I'm gonna smash that arseface of yours.

'Arseface in the first degree.'

And before I could think, No, maybe better not, I'd punched his nose, right there in the middle of that big ugly crack. I don't know how but my arm was faster than my thoughts, a solid hit before I even realised it myself, as if my body had decided to seek justice on its own.

Notebooks flying to the ground, shedding pages like trees in autumn, and suddenly I'm shedding an old image of myself and speaking openly to Arseface, whose eyes goggle like someone who can't believe his own eyes, his own ears, his own runny nose.

'You'll pay for this.'

'Sure I will. Let this be a lesson to you, Arseface.'

I muttered to myself while the others stood by speechless in admiration; suddenly I felt ten centimetres taller.

But now I can't react any more; I have to be careful not to draw attention to myself. I speed up. Arseface pretends not to see me, and yet I pass so close to him I can count his moles like pistachios in his nasty mortadella face, one by one. I speed up, and I'm past. Almost home.

Mama's still sleeping, buried between the pillows.

Seeing her like that in the big bed, she seems smaller. Still the same expression, just her face is darker. When I touch her she seems colder. But so is outside. I put a coat over her, two euros fall out of one of the pockets. It's hard to get back up from the blankets.

If people are happy they don't die like this, just by chance.

Maybe they die in an accident, but not in their sleep.

Maybe Mama died of heart problems, because no one could love her enough, not even me. Maybe I wasn't able to make her stay in my life, to make her live for me at least. Maybe I'm not worth much at all, not for her, not for anyone. I take off my shoes with this new idea spinning in my head. I hurl one shoe here, another one there. Blue is scared. He makes his tail big so that it looks like that fluffy thing for getting rid of spiderwebs. One shoe ends up under the sofa. I've got titicaca in my socks. I have to accept my responsibilities.

What are my responsibilities?

Keep my room clean, check to make sure the cat is OK, change his litter, study, don't say 'fucking shit' all the time, be sure the gas is off if I've used the oven. Do what I need to do so there isn't food between my teeth.

Don't be an extra bump in the road when the going gets tough.

Understand that grown-ups have grown-up problems.

Adults have no idea how many strategies kids have to come up with to be what they are. Sometimes they tell you to stop acting like a child, other times that it doesn't matter because you're just a child . . . but what a beautiful child! What a little man. I think about the little coat-hanger men who hold up the clothes in the wardrobe that smell like mothballs. Because I close myself in there I might become a little hanger man myself, with bony shoulders and a question-mark head. Who knows?

In any case, even adults don't always know what they're saying.

'I'm drawing a blank.'

Or: 'Funeral for the deceased.'

Who else would it be for?

I go into my room to look for my slippers, the ones

with the moose horns that Mama gave me for Christmas. Blue's chewed on them, so now one horn is leaking yellow cotton wool, like the stuff they put up your nose when it's bleeding. Like when I got hit in the face with the football and they took me to A&E. Mama thought it was a concussion and was more upset than I was, but they told her it was nothing.

As I slipper across the room Blue tries to grab what's left of the horn. On TV the chef is still there, surrounded by women all dressed up and being all over the top – I zap them. In the kitchen the table and the floor are covered with cat biscuits; I forgot to put the box away and Blue has scattered them everywhere. The sink is full of dirty dishes. On the windowsill there's a plant Mama calls a succulent, a gift from someone or other, made up of two kinds of spiny cucumbers, one tall and one short. It survives even without water, like us. We're succulents too, shut up in the house. If you touch it it stings in self-defence.

The house like this makes me sick.

It's not like when you're alone for a day and you do what you want, and what you usually can't. Now I can do everything and I don't feel like doing anything. I'm so free my head spins just thinking about it. I'm free and I'm a prisoner at the same time, like hamsters that spin their wheels and stay in the same place. They spin and spin and don't go anywhere.

If I stop for a moment the blank notebook comes back into my head and I can't even imagine. It's horrible because it's thanks to daydreams that I've always made it through OK. Teachers say I have a vivid imagination.

'Imagination is a great resource in times like these. Perhaps you're unaware of this because you don't read newspapers, but at times reality is stranger than fantasy. So it becomes necessary to be even more fantastic in order to make it in life.'

But now I don't know what to imagine.

I imagine that this whole thing is happening to someone else, because it's a bit like that: I'm inside what's happening but also outside; I want to disappear but at the same time I don't. I don't feel like shutting myself up in the wardrobe any more, because now everything is like a closed wardrobe, but also like an open one – there's no point in hiding inside the house any more. I can whine and wipe my nose on the tablecloth, the napkins, my pyjamas, the curtains in the living room. Everything is old. It all smells like an old wardrobe. Wide open and sealed shut at the same time. I can do everything and I don't want anything – I only want to go back to how it was. I bury my nose in the last piece of toilet paper. I make myself a Nutella sandwich. The bottle of milk is empty. I drink the tap water, which tastes like chlorine.

In winter the days are short, but today seems to go on for ever, an endless incomprehensible eternity.

I don't even understand if I should give up hope or not.

'Hope is the last to die.'

Or the second to last?

Mama seems more and more dead.

I should study the history of hominids, those slouching, hairy creatures in our textbooks, walking in single file until one straightens up and marches ahead like a soldier: *forward* march.

With a hominid around maybe Mama would feel less lonely.

'Why is it you can't make up your mind to find a decent man?' Giulia asks her. 'I say this for your son's sake as well, because you can't do it all alone.'

'I'm tired of falling in love, tired of falling out of love, tired of fucking. I don't even remember how to make love any more.'

'That's love! Right now things seem one way to you, but that's not necessarily the way things are. Look at me. I've been falling in and out of love since I was fifteen. Every time I say never again: may I be struck down if I fall for it again. Then I meet another one, and it's another round, another race. If you find one who knows what he's about, you'll see how quickly you change your mind.'

'No, for me it's different. To fall in love you need to want it, and I just want to sleep.'

Mama lights another cigarette and curls a lock of hair round her finger. Giulia just sits there with her nose in the air, contemplating the smoke as it curls round itself, in search of inspiration or else the right moment to slip away.

I may as well deactivate my periaudio since certain conversations have been interrupted for who knows how long, trailing so many little dots behind.

Sometimes Giulia invites her out to dinner with friends and Mama invents an excuse that is usually me.

'Sorry, this evening I really have to stay home with him. You know how he is . . .'

Other times Mama says she suffers from loneliness.

'Loneliness is a whistling that worms itself into your head. It's the echo of ships that have already sailed, which you can no longer reach, not even if you swim.'

She told me: 'Once a ship or a train departs there's

nothing else you can do. You're left gazing after a gleam of light on the horizon, slowly fading into the fog, the way a memory fades into the dull grey of the present.'

She says: 'That's how I feel, like I'm on the shore, or in an empty station, having arrived too late to life.'

Mama feels lonely even though she's never alone, because I'm always here with her, but it must not be enough. In order not to feel so lonely she went to talk to a man with a beard, who listens to her once a week in a house full of books full of complicated thoughts. I flipped through a few of them while I waited in the lobby. I wonder though, what do you get out of paying someone to listen to you, to care for you?

I care for her for free, but it must not be enough.

It may be that she doesn't want to confess her darkest thoughts to me directly. Sometimes she writes them down using tiny, tiny letters, then forgets the pieces of paper on the kitchen table; or else talks about them to somebody in a low voice. She talks slowly and she moves slowly.

She did it the other night too.

At times Mama moves in slow motion.

When she slows down more than usual she decides not to go to work for a few days.

'One of these days they'll end up firing me.'

I think one of these days came.

So she took a day or two to sleep.

When normal people don't work they go on holiday.

Last year even Mama took a week of real holiday and we went to Venice.

'Do you know that if you go to Venice with a man before you're married, then you won't ever marry him? It happened to me once.'

Or more than once.

More than a city, Venice seems like one of those books with three-dimensional objects that pop out of the pages, suddenly spreading out before your eyes. You turn the corner and you feel like you're turning a page, like you're falling into another fantastic story. Venice is all hand-drawn. The houses are ancient and every detail of the façades seems specially designed by an architect in a wizard's hat. There are no cars and you can walk everywhere. Gondolas slip by on the water, each one piloted by a single sailor with a striped shirt like mine.

Mama and I took a ride around like the couples do.

'Don't you think this city's magical? Isn't it incredible that places like this still exist in the world?'

We went to visit the churches and the museums with their paintings that are hundreds of years old, where you have to whisper so you don't disturb the others. In one we discovered a special place under an arch where everyone sticks their gum. We stopped and played under the portico of a palazzo on the canal: if you can walk round the base of one of the columns without falling you get to make a wish. Almost nobody makes it, but it's fun to try.

'Don't say it, don't tell me the wish. If you say it then it won't come true.'

We bought a glass ashtray and wrote postcards while we sat at a little café table with the glittering sea in front of us and to one side a church with a golden ball on top: to Giulia, to Grandma, to Davide and Chubby Broccolo, plus I sent Antonella one with a gondola. I wrote 'Greetings from Venice'. I wanted to write 'I love you' but was too embarrassed.

We had some really good gelato. It was like a bar of chocolate dipped in whipped cream. The waiter recommended it to us and Mama said, 'Sure, let's try it. We're on holiday, and it's always a good idea to try the local speciality.'

It must be wonderful to live in a place like Venice.

I wonder how it would have been if my stork had been re-routed and I'd been born in Venice.

'In winter though, Venice is depressing.'

So no then, I think it's better how it is, for us to be where we are.

Mama says that in winter Venice is like a cold: the world outside is even more muffled and faraway, and your head pounds for no reason while your nose runs, like those stray cats with heart-shaped noses that nobody has the heart to clean.

But the thing I remember most in Venice is that it's either extremely noisy or extremely quiet. Either you're walking in the middle of millions of people who are stepping on your feet and getting stuck in the really narrow streets or on the bridges, and everyone's shouting in different languages and the gondoliers are singing and the boats' motors are roaring and there's always someone hammering somewhere, or there's a radio going or people calling out to each other from one place to another, or else you take a random turn and maybe you find an open space where there's nobody, and the only thing you can hear is the water in the canals and the echo of your footsteps, or the calls of seagulls chasing each other. It's like suddenly being in another world, but all this happens by chance, because you don't really know where you are; you're just lost again. It's a happy silence though, not like the one now.

*   *   *

I'm listening to the silence when suddenly my periaudio picks up a signal: a shuffle of footsteps behind the door. Waves of blood crash in my head, whipping up a storm. I listen some more: there's someone moving. I hear a creak like when Mama gets out of bed and scrapes her feet around on the ground in search of her slippers, which is like the flapping of a moth caught inside a lampshade.

It can't be true. I hope so much that it's true. I hope with all my might that it's Mama, Mama who's finally decided to get up and return to us. Like the people who remember their entire past life a moment before they die, in a second I see the rest of my life to come, now that we're about to go back to living. Like when I heard a friendly, cracking voice booming from the flat next door, and I hoped it wasn't our neighbour but someone much nearer, the nearest kind of neighbour, one who sings in the shower or while shaving, sings love songs or opera for Mama, but also for me.

I listen again.

The noises become clearer. I make out two voices, voices of people I don't know. The neighbour who loved opera moved away two years ago.

I prayed to Mama for it to be true, but it's not true.

The noises aren't coming from Mama's room. There's someone muttering behind the front door.

I don't even have time to think before I hear someone ring the bell.

Once, twice.

Who could it be at this hour? How did they manage to get into the building? How'd they find me out? I've been silent as a mouse the whole time.

I hold my breath as I bring my eye to the peephole, as slowly as I can, like a burglar in reverse, one who's afraid of being discovered living in his own house.

I see two decrepit old women, all bundled up against the cold. Blue starts to miaow.

'We're Jehovah's Witnesses. Is there anyone home?'

'No, it's just a cat. Let's go.'

3

Today Antonella has a ponytail.

And a hair clip shaped like a ladybird. If a ladybird lands on you it's a sign of good luck. I'd like to be older, to be able to go to the cinema with her alone, to sit in the back row and give her a kiss. Usually when I think of something impossible it distracts me, then everything goes back to normal: peace, amen.

But today's different.

It's like with a toothache. If it goes away for five minutes it seems like you never had it. But then the pain yanks you back, and it seems like all you have is teeth, like you're just one giant tooth, and you can't think of anything else. You become your tooth; nothing else is important to you. You'd like to have dentures and put them in a glass on the bedside table like Grandpa. The dentures smile all on their own and you don't have to think about it any more. You don't even have to try.

It's like the rain, the kind of rain that gives you no hope it'll ever stop. The trees have disappeared in some kind of fuzzy mist. They're plane trees, the kind that motorists smash into.

Chubby Broccolo is looking out of the window too.

Chubby is great, but never ask him for a bite of his sandwich.

Chubby's real name is Francesco, but only the grown-ups call him Francesco, when they have to tell him off.

Mama says that obese children will have millions of problems when they grow up. I'm not obese but I have millions of problems right now.

I think I'm fairly good-looking, because everyone says so.

'You're the spitting image of your mother.'

Davide asks me if I'll go to the cinema with him that afternoon.

'It's Elisabetta's birthday so we're all going to the cinema.'

'Sounds great. I'll call you after lunch.'

'Will your mother let you?'

'I think I can convince her.'

'I'll tell my mother to call yours,' he says.

Fucking shit, I think.

'OK,' I say.

I'll make up something later, I think.

It's hard to behave so that no one suspects anything, when they don't know anything.

With one part of my brain I listen to the lesson about hominids, all the stages of the evolution of man leading up to *Homo sapiens*, which would be us now. With the other part I think of a solution, because I'd like to go to the cinema; if nothing else it would distract me.

I don't even know if I really want to go to the cinema with them but I do want everything to be normal. And it would be normal to go to the cinema with Davide and his pain-in-the-arse of a sister.

I wonder what it must be like to have a sister, and if it's better to have an older or a younger one, like Davide's sister Elisabetta. I've thought about it so many times without reaching any conclusion. There are pros and cons.

Right now, for example, it would be a disaster. Sisters don't know how to keep their mouths shut because they're girls and they think they know how to do everything. Davide's sister always butts in, always acting like she knows more about things. Then if you figure out that seven times eight equals fifty-six before she does, she starts to scream the house down because she can't stand losing. When she makes biscuits we all have to eat them and they're awful, super hard like nougat but without the nougat flavour. It's like munching on a pencil and I hate pencils even when they're shaped like biscuits. I hate pencils because even if you rub out what you've done, underneath there's always still a dark mark. Then again if I had a smart, well-trained sister, a sister that was all mine, it would be better because at least then I'd have someone to talk to.

I can't decide about this sister thing. Maybe a brother would be better, I don't know. But even then it would depend on the brother. Maybe a twin – a twin would definitely think about things the same way.

To distract myself I do the breathing exercise, to see how long I can go without breathing, every time a little longer.

I hold my breath until I almost suffocate, looking at the hands of the clock. It's a kind of video game, except you play it just with yourself. Every time you try to beat the last time. The great thing is that you can also do it at school and nobody notices.

Once when I was doing the breathing exercise Mrs Squarzetti asked me, 'What is the capital of France?' I looked at her with my eyes popping out of my head because I was about to explode, but I couldn't give up.

'Are you feeling all right?'

I beat the old record and shouted, 'Paris!'

spluttering on my notebook, saying Paris as if it had lots of 'P's. There's still a mark where my spit dissolved the ink.

'Well done!' she'd said, terribly pleased with herself.

I know, I know, I thought.

I'd like to have a timer so I could time myself more accurately. I also like to write with my left hand. I'm training to be able to write with both hands like Leonardo da Vinci, who was a genius. But the writing looks like it's Blue's or maybe the doctor's. If I write coming from the other direction you can't understand anything.

'Yeah, you're right. Absolutely nothing's going right today.'

But can I go to the cinema with Davide and his mother and his sister anyway? Today's Elisabetta's birthday. Can I? It's true that you can't go, but what about me? Can I? Please, let me go. It's an amazing film, it could even help with school. If I go you won't be cross? And you're not just saying you won't get cross but then you'll get cross anyway? Because I'm a little cross too, you know. I know it's not your fault. But I don't like to come home like this; the house is too quiet when you don't talk. I can't talk with anyone. Maybe I could talk with Giulia. Do you think that's a good idea? That she'll understand? That she could help us? That we can trust her? That she knows how to keep a secret? That she's capable of understanding us? That if she understood us she'd find a solution? That there is a solution? That it will be over soon? That Giulia will call while she's on holiday? That you're worth something to her? That it's better if we sort things out on our own, like always? That we'll know how to sort things out? That we don't need anyone else? That I can do it? Do you think so?

Otherwise I could call the vet who is a kind of doctor at least, but I don't know if that's a good idea.

I'm really not sure what to do. I'll end up not doing anything.

I could talk to a friend, but I don't know if I have such a friendly friend. Anyway, friends are crawling with parents. If they let anything slip out I'm finished.

'It's all right, Mama, don't worry. Everything went fine at school, as usual.'

I head down the hall.

'Do you think it's my fault you died?'

I have to call Davide, to tell him about the cinema.

'My mother said it's fine, she'll drop me off. What time?'

'At four.'

'OK, see you at your place.'

Luckily I know where Davide lives. I'll have to take the tram, but it's easy.

The people on the tram stink. It's always that way when it rains. The coats smell like wet dog. Or car seats when people have smoked there. Every once in a while adults stink. They've got bad breath or hair that smells like unmade beds. Old people stink of old people. My grandpa stunk of really old people. He was really old. Grandma smells like violets and lilies of the valley, like linen forgotten in a drawer. Mama was born by accident when Grandma thought she couldn't have any more children because she was already on pause.

'It was a miracle I was born, or a joke, you know? A joke of nature.'

At the third stop I get off.

I arrive at Davide's house and ring the bell.

'My mother was in a hurry because she had to go to the doctor.'

I go up.

Davide's house isn't bad. It's always a bit crazy. Better than Marco's house, where right away the maid makes you feel uncomfortable and everything is in its place, with the newspapers and books on the tables fanned out like in a doctor's waiting room and you already feel sick, already sure they'll find something wrong with you: Hmm, exactly as I suspected, try to cough a little. People who are perfect always make you feel like rubbish.

Davide's mother, on the other hand, always seems a bit disorganised. She wears long scarves and never goes to the hairdresser's. She's always waving her arms around as if she's chasing away flies. She's agitated now too, so she's not worried about Mama not being able to come up. We have a Coke and then go to the cinema to see *Ice Age*.

The film isn't bad, it's just that all I can think about is what I'll do afterwards; I have to make sure I get a lift without making them suspicious. During the intermission Davide tells me that tomorrow he's going to come to my place to do homework. This sends me into total panic, so I don't catch much of what happened to the prehistoric animals. For me a new age has dawned: we've entered the late Liar era.

They always tell you that you shouldn't tell lies, but without lies I'd already be in an orphanage.

This, in any case, is my first true lie.

It's no use crossing my fingers or my toes or touching my nose for luck. I don't have any choice. It's just that in the movies at least you always have someone else to face the tough times with. There's a main character in difficulty and at a certain point someone appears to get him out of trouble. Maybe I shouldn't have come to the cinema, but it was for the sake of the details: someone who goes to the cinema can't have a mother dead in her bed.

Luckily when we leave, Davide's sister is wailing that she wants to go and eat hamburgers right now. She makes such a racket that no one wonders why I'm so quiet.

'Do you want to come with us?'

'No, I can't, my mother's waiting for me. Actually she asked if you could give me a lift since she didn't know what time she'd be done at the doctor's.'

'Do you want us to call her?'

'No, when she's at the doctor's she turns her phone off.'

I feel like a genius. A genius who has just fallen from the eighth floor and landed without a scratch because they were moving mattresses below, one of those crazy news stories that pop up in the papers every so often, when reality is stranger than fantasy.

'Child Falls from Window, Lands on Guide Dog, nearly Pulls Blind Man under Tram: No One Hurt.' Grandma loved that kind of thing.

Or else I'm like cats with their nine lives; they leap off the balcony to catch a pigeon and miraculously survive.

We get in their car and five minutes later we're in front of my house. Elisabetta says to me, 'Too bad for you, you can't come and eat with us.'

I stick out my tongue at her.

Davide says, 'See you tomorrow.'

His mother: 'Bye, dear.' And then she says some dirty word to the guy complaining that we're double parked.

They wait for me to get in the front door. I don't turn to wave goodbye.

When I hear the car leaving I think maybe I've gone too far. Someone goes to the cinema, comes home, and at home there's still Mama dead in her bed.

It's not possible.

It doesn't make sense.

It's just a story I made up to frighten myself.

I like to read. I read without stumbling over the words, even when I have to read out loud, even when Grandma would make me get up on the chair and Mama would scold her.

'For heaven's sake, we're not at the circus.'

I would stand there in my pyjamas, barefoot like a parrot clutching at my perch, and recite Manzoni – 'He has passed, As stark and still' – and I really was still, until the end of the poem.

Words are wonderful because there are so many.

Best of all I like difficult and long words like 'antidisestablishmentarianism'.

Or funny ones, like 'topsy-turvy'. There are lots of ways to talk about a huge confusion but topsy-turvy is my favourite. So on the walls of the Year 1 classrooms, along with the word 'aeroplane' in the shape of an aeroplane and 'banana' in the shape of a banana, they could attach a photo of me and Mama as 'topsy' and 'turvy', the one where we look just like each other, like two peas in a pod, held together tight-tight in our shell.

Words are useful to work out what others are really saying, the ones who think you can't understand.

Words in a row make stories.

You put things in a row and make a story out of it. Stories put things in their places. Then you're more relaxed. The stories you invent are your personal lullabies. Even when they're horrible they don't scare you any more because you're the one who invented them.

That's what this is too.

This story is only a secret I told myself to see if I'm able to keep a really secret secret.

Now I open the door and smell meatballs in the hall.

Meatballs and mash, my favourite, the meal Mama makes me when she has to ask me to forgive her for something big.

She's still there.

Usually she helps me do my homework. Or she checks it afterwards. Or else she listens while I recite something in English. It seems like English is very important. English is useful for songs and for PlayStation too. If you know English you understand certain things better.

Tomorrow I have a test at school.

No matter what, I have to study.

I have to study, study, study.

If you don't study, friend, you're fucked. If you don't get at least a 'Good' on this fucking test, you're shit out of luck. They'll put a big black mark next to your name and call a fucking parents meeting.

Do you get it, friend? Dear Mama will have to go and talk to the arsefaces who are talking behind your back. Who will you send, friend – the cat?

'Fucking shit, Blue, let's get to work. Let's show those arsefaces who we are.'

Careful, friend, if you use dirty words they'll fuck you up.

'OK, OK,' I say, and put on my tough-guy face. 'We'll be the ones doing the fucking up around here, friend.'

No problem.

4

Something is different today.

Mama has gone hard and swollen all over. Yesterday she was colder; today she's puffier. I try touching the radiator to see if it's working – it's not. Mama's not working any more either.

There's a layer of dust on the radiator. She hasn't noticed. Now it's all the same for her if things are dirty or clean, ugly or pretty, lukewarm, freezing, or just terrible. She's finished fighting with opposites.

My heart starts beating loudly. I can feel it in my belly and in my head, like a pinball racing wildly, smacking randomly into the walls of my body, elbowing me in the stomach, battering me with punches to the sides of my head, pounding my back, filling me with bruises and shivers. I can't stop it doing whatever it wants, shooting all over the place.

Today I stopped hoping.

I look around and nothing seems like before.

I don't even know if there was a before.

I don't know if there will be an after.

I don't know anything about anything.

The blank notebook still covers my whole brain. This has to be how crazy people feel, in their white padded cells, rocking from side to side, staring into the sum of all colours.

I'm rocking too, without even feeling like crying. I just feel like rocking back and forth on the edge of the bed.

'Mama's lost her spark, her mouth is oh so dark, no playing in the park . . .'

I don't know where the song comes from, I'm not the one who's thinking it. It's the song that's thinking me.

'Forget. Forgot. Forgotten.'

'Forgive. Forgave. Forgiven'

We listen to the verbs recited aloud and parrot them back. Then we have to complete sentences using the correct verb. My desk-mate tries to copy me, but I'm in a daze, with my pen in the air. I hear the sound of the words without understanding what they mean, like Ulysses with the Sirens, but to me they seem like police sirens.

'What's up with you? Are you daydreaming? What goes here?'

'Where?'

'Here! Third line: "forget" or "forgotten"?'

'It's the same thing.'

No, it's not the same thing.

I don't want to end up in a home. 'Forget,' I write, and elbow my desk-mate. The torture is over. I get up to hand in the test.

I hope I did well. I think I did.

I walk towards the front to hand in my notebook and it seems like I weigh a hundred kilograms. I know I weigh less than half that, but it's as if I'm made of reinforced concrete, with a stone heart inside. I feel I can only move like King Tut's mummy, completely stiff. I feel the floor give way as if it can't support me, or maybe it's my knees that have suddenly gone mushy. I feel everything and nothing. But somehow I reach the finish line, and force myself to smile. It's exactly like when you leave the dentist after having held your mouth wide open for two hours – it stays stuck like that and forgets how to move. My cheeks are sore.

'Very good.'

It appears everything is going well, very well.

The bell rings and we're free once more.

Davide wants to come to my house after lunch.

'Great,' I say.

He says he'll bring *Snowboarding*.

'Even better,' I say.

I go back home. I plan my journey carefully, choosing the opposite side of the road from where the flower woman sets up, so she won't get a chance to talk my ear off. I watch her across the street as she uses her poultry shears to cut down the stems of some lilies. She's got mean eyes and big, wrinkly hands. Until not too long ago she always used to give me a little pat when Mama and I stopped to buy flowers, little bunches of irises that smelled like bubble bath.

'Is this a gift, madam?'

'No, they're for me.'

'Shall I put a bow on it?'

'No, thanks, that won't be necessary.'

Every time the same questions and the same answers. Mama tries not to pay attention to the old busybody. She drops a coin or her wallet on purpose, or she fixes her hair like it's no big deal and swallows a few times before saying goodbye. Then the flower woman's hand touches my forehead, and it feels like having the bottom of a shoe on my face, or a bare foot with warty calluses.

I don't understand old people's obsession with

touching children. They should keep at least as far away as the years separating us.

I walk past as far away as possible.

But I could, I should, I would like to buy some flowers for Mama, because people bring flowers to the dead. People bring flowers to their lovers, to sick people, and to the dead (there's not a whole lot of common sense in all this).

Mama likes white irises, or red roses.

'It may be a cliché, but if a man buys you red roses it still makes you happy.'

I know what she means: I don't have to be a woman. It's that it's important to feel important to somebody.

People are ashamed of not feeling loved enough.

People always keep themselves to themselves. If someone thinks about you enough to send you roses, it means that they think about you a lot, that you're not alone. It's more or less the same with all presents. Actually, that's what presents are. That's why they matter even if they're not worth much. It's the thought that counts, they say, and about this they're right.

Tomorrow I'll buy her some beautiful flowers, the most beautiful flowers she's ever had, but not today. I can't deal with the old witch and her questions and her sandpaper touch.

The last time Mama got flowers it made her very happy. It was a bunch of red roses so big it didn't fit through the door, and there was a little card attached with a pin. In her rush to read it Mama pricked her finger, then fell into a trance like Sleeping Beauty for a couple of days.

To be honest she'd seemed happy for a while before then, strangely enough, and a bit absent-minded. She bustled around in high heels, tic-tac tic-tac, and acted like someone who's just got away with something. That was a couple of years ago. The night before the roses she'd left me at home with the babysitter with the big boobs, Juana, and stayed out late. I'd fallen asleep on the sofa between Juana's boobs, soft as a mattress, and Juana fell asleep too because it was past midnight.

When Juana heard the key turn in the lock she was really embarrassed.

'*Lo siento*, *señora*, but I've been up since six in the morning, so sorry.'

Juana's boobs trembled like jellies with a cherry on top, but Mama didn't even notice.

'Don't worry, dear, it's nothing to worry about. I'm the one who's late. It's my fault.'

Mama seemed more concerned with looking at herself in the mirror above the chest of drawers than with us, as if some detail might have revealed why she was late. And in fact when Mama returned to the flat she had a ladder in her stockings on the right ankle – before leaving she'd had one on her left. I'd tried to warn her.

'One should never arrive at an appointment with torn stockings. If you have an accident and have to take your clothes off, who knows what they'll think of you.'

But she'd been too busy getting ready to go out.

She apologised again, even gave the babysitter a tip, and came to kiss me goodnight. Her perfume was different than usual, sharper. It smelled like the little green trees people hang in their cars.

It didn't last long.

After a few days the petals fell on the table and also on the floor. As Mama bent down on all fours to pick them up among the chair legs, she declared that when the roses wilt quickly it means that it wasn't true love.

Whose love she meant I never asked her.

In any case, that was one of the few times I ever saw her truly happy.

Or at least happy about red roses.

Maybe she's happy again now.

The light part of her has left her body and the heavy part has stayed in bed, like with a puppet. The puppets' stories exist even when they're sleeping. And even when people die their stories still exist.

Once I had a high temperature and I thought it was chicken pox because the next day I had itchy blisters everywhere. I was in bed, but also out of bed.

I saw myself from the outside. I moved around the room, obsessed with finding something, a bow and arrow, which should have been between the door and the wardrobe, along with the tennis racket. I had to hit an important target, that's what I needed it for, but I couldn't find it, and if I found it I couldn't manage to pick it up, because my body was in bed. Only my will to pick up the bow was moving around the room, and my will had no hands to grab things with. It was separate from me, me who remained stretched out on the bed, mouthing words that made no sound or sense.

Mama says she needs lightness.

'But every day things are getting heavier. Even the atmosphere at work is getting heavy.'

Giulia raises her eyes to the heavens.

'What can you do? The fact is they're arseholes, every last one of them. Sure, if you hadn't ended up alone with Luca you could have kept painting instead of working in that stupid office, but not with a kid on your back.'

Mama makes a sign for her to keep her voice down.

'What's Luca got to do with it? If they're arseholes they're arseholes.'

But I understand; it's not easy to paint with someone on your back. Still, I thought then that maybe if Mama stopped working and rested at least for a little while, things would go better. Maybe if she stopped working she'd go back to being an artist and paint something better than what we've got hanging up in the living room.

Will there be any fruit juice left for when Davide comes round?

I'll tell him Mama's at work, but it'll seem strange if the fridge is empty and there's nothing for a snack. We need a little snack and some juice, at least.

Supplies will run out sooner or later and Blue will end up with an empty bowl. Poor guy. It's amazing how such a small cat can eat so much.

The kitchen looks awful, like when you get home after being away for a while. I don't think Davide will mind. His house is always a mess, worse than here. Good thing there are some leftovers in the fridge at least.

I eat some gelato. Sometimes when Davide comes over he brings something. As long as it's not his sister's biscuits, the ones shaped like hearts or stars that look great but then eating them means breaking a tooth.

I go and lock the door to Mama's room with Mama inside.

If Davide wants to go in there I'll say that Mama doesn't want anyone to, because I looked in her drawers. That's why her room is locked. It's not completely a lie, it's even half true, because I really did go looking in her drawers a few weeks ago. I wanted to read what she'd written the night before. She'd stayed up writing in the living room until late and I wanted to know what was really on her mind. She seemed in a worse mood than usual.

I didn't find the pages. I found stockings, underwear and a pink thing shaped like a willy hidden underneath the stockings and underwear.

You push a button and the thing turns on and goes vrrrrr, like a blender.

Mama went through the roof.

'Don't you ever dare lay your hands on my things again.'

On your pink thing, I thought, but didn't say it, because she was angry enough already.

I didn't even tell her what I was looking for and why; it seemed impossible to straighten things out. I started to sweat like it was the middle of August.

'Have I ever come nosing around in your room? Have I ever opened your shitty private box where you keep all your junk? Have I ever spied on you?'

Who knows? I thought. I don't think so.

'Then why do you do it to me? What happened to all the respect I've taught you? Go on, tell me that!'

Mama screamed like a madwoman.

'Don't use dirty words, Mama.'

'Who? Me? Fuck you and fuck everyone!'

Usually she doesn't yell, but that time she went for it.

She had a handkerchief in her hands, like the ones she keeps in the drawer on top of the pink thing, which she was clutching so tightly it seemed like she might rip it to shreds at any moment, as if the whole world could crumble to pieces in an instant. For the first time I saw her veins climb up from her fists to her wrists, bluish and swollen. They were no longer my mother's hands but my grandmother's, or a man's, a demon-possessed Australian-Aboriginal mechanic. Mama didn't seem like Mama any more; she seemed like a really pissed-off stranger, capable of anything.

The next morning she muttered, 'Sorry.'

I kept staring at my cup and the teddy bear – shaped biscuits as I dipped them into the milk.

'Sorry, there was no reason to get so angry about it.'

What a shitty excuse, what a shitty life, what a shitty everything.

That time Mama managed to make me feel just like a fucking shit. Why she would keep a pretend willy in her underwear drawer is still a mystery; maybe it was a tacky gift she got from her colleagues as a joke, beats me.

A disgusting mystery, to be honest.

I never thought about my mother like the women in dirty magazines. And I don't want to think about it.

Sometimes, in secret, Davide and I look at dirty magazines. His dad keeps them on top of a wardrobe, along with some films too, because he thinks no one can get up there. On top of the magazines there's a suitcase, and on top of the suitcase a bag with pliers, wrenches, screwdrivers and other men's things inside. Davide gives me a boost and I climb up because I'm lighter, while his fingers get red and swollen like sausages in the packet. My willy has much pinker skin than the ones in the pictures. Maybe they get darker as they grow, the opposite of hair.

It's not that I don't know that Mama likes to have sex once in a while. I'm sure that she did with the last one, the one whose job seemed to be washing windscreens at traffic lights.

'*Vade retro*, *Satana*,' she'd cry out in her little girl's voice.

'Vade retro!'

I'd hear her Vaderetros from behind the door when I went to pee during the night. Once in a while I'd also hear her laugh and I'd think, at least she's laughing. They have sex because, for some mysterious reason, they like each other. It doesn't have anything to with that other stuff.

The fact remains that now the room is closed, with Mama dead inside, and Davide mustn't notice anything.

When he arrives he says there's a funny smell.

'I don't smell anything,' I reply.

We play with Blue for a bit. Davide scratches him on the belly and Blue sticks his paws up in the air, like a dog.

'I told you a cat isn't so different from a dog.'

'Why is Blue called Blue, when he's grey?'

What a moronic question.

'Why are you called Davide, when you're a moron?'

We end up in a fight.

'Stop it, you're hurting me! You're hurting me, ouch!'

I'm hitting him for real, not playing any more. I'm

on top of him and I'm holding him down with a strength I've never had before. He's shouting and slapping his hand down on the carpet like in judo.

'I surrender, I surrender.'

I realise I don't want to let go. I apologise.

'Sorry, I didn't mean to hurt you.'

'What did you do that for?'

It's never happened before. Davide is much bigger than me. It's better with *Snowboard* – he wins. I keep falling; I get the buttons confused; I can't get it right. I see the turn coming and can't help trying some fancy move, so I fly into the air and off the course, onto the roof of the chalet. The spectators laugh. Davide complains because he says playing like that is no fun. We drink fruit juice. And eat the last of the snacks.

'What do you say we do some homework?'

'Fine, I'll do it for you.'

It's always like this, we do homework and then I do it for him. It's because it's easier for me, I don't know why.

'You know, it's handy having a friend who's a swot.'

'If you don't like it, we can go back to fighting.'

'Arsehole.'

'Whoever says so is a hundred times more than me.'

'You want me to give you a Chinese burn?'

He twists the skin on my wrist with both his hands until I'm the one who yells.

Mama says it's because I was born at seven months and seven-month babies are more intelligent. I was in an incubator for two months. Maybe I've fallen back in, because once again I find myself in an evil machine that creates horrible nightmares, and I'm still too small to get out and get away on my own. I don't even know if it's true that seven-month babies are more gifted. In any case I only want to be normal.

Even if sometimes it's useful to understand things first.

At seven o'clock Davide's mother buzzes.

He thinks it's my mother, but I know it's his. It has to be.

'He'll be right down,' I say into the intercom.

'C'mon, get a move on, move, hurry,' I tell Davide, pushing him out the door.

Friday night: taiga and tundra in the house.

Titicaca more or less everywhere.

I turn the key in the lock to Mama's room and peek in. I think about the door in *The Texas Chainsaw Massacre 2* and decide to leave it wide open.

Maybe there really is a funny smell. Maybe it's the

toilet. Every so often it stinks, because of the low pressure, Mama says.

Low pressure over the entire Mediterranean basin, but people don't seem to be any less stressed.

I turn on every light. In the freezer I find two fish fingers. I look at the best before date – it's already passed. Doesn't matter. It wasn't that long ago. I put them in a pan with oil; I have to cook them for five minutes a side.

I'm not even so sure I'm hungry.

But I feel like I have to feed myself, so I don't waste away, don't get sick, don't get taken away.

In orphanages the orphans always eat the same soup, it's take it or leave it. I'd be happy to only eat fish fingers, chips, pizza, prosciutto and mash and meatballs. It's not really the same thing though.

In orphanages you have to eat like all the other kids and with all the other kids, play with all the other kids and sleep with all the other kids, even if you're not tired. From what I can tell in orphanages you can never do anything different.

I'm not used to that. I'm used to living with Mama and our life is different from others people's.

You can be equal, normal or different.

Equal is when you have to be like others. Normal is

when you get to do great stuff everyone likes. Different is when you have a bit of a strange life, which is definitely not equal but neither is it normal; it's a life that's a bit lonely, a bit on its own, just like ours.

Normal is the best of all, but different is better than dead equal.

Equal is a bit like the sky when it's grey all over, like the bottom of the non-stick pan.

'Don't scratch it or you'll poison yourself.'

Don't climb over the gate or you'll end up stuck like a chicken kebab. Don't climb over the barbed-wire fence or you'll get tetanus. Don't jump on the mattress or the whole thing will collapse. Don't stay out late or I'll be worried. Don't cross the street without looking. Don't eat like a caveman. Don't put your elbows on the table. Don't talk to people you don't know. Don't trust people – hey, what are you doing?

Nothing! Just frying some fish fingers!

At the smell of fish Blue launches himself like an earth-to-air missile onto the kitchen counter, knocking over the bottle of oil, which spills everywhere, and Blue slips and slides like in the cartoons, which makes me laugh out loud.

It's not funny. He looks at me like he's really telling me off.

'True, but it still really makes me laugh.'

When the sky is like that, all grey and indifferent, everything sliding right off its back, you don't think it can ever change. When it's sunny with a few clouds, that's normal. When it's stormy it's bad, but it's also beautiful.

With Mama it's like always living in a moment before the storm: you don't know if it will come, but you know it could. Some nights you even hope it will, just so you don't have to be on guard the whole time.

Now the storm is here and we're all about to drown, but Blue and I are still bobbing along. Cats don't even like water. They don't let cats into orphanages.

I don't like having baths. But I have to have them, because if I stink they might say: 'It's a bit fishy when such a clean boy starts to smell.'

When Blue fell into the bathtub once he looked like he'd stuck his paws in an electric socket. Don't put your paws in the socket or you'll get electrocuted; don't stick your fingers in your nose; don't stick your nose in other people's business – but he won't fall for it again.

'Believe me, a hot bath always does you good. You soak a bit and then you feel like new.'

I turn on the bath taps and sit on the toilet. I check down there to see if there is any lichen or moss growing

– there isn't, but when I sniff my hand it smells like cheese. I pour bubble bath into the water, the one that makes lots of foam. I take off my clothes and realise that my feet have joined the Blackfoot Indians. The mirror is all fogged up; with my finger I write 'fucking shit'. I get in the bath. At first the water is hot, then it cools down. My willy floats in the water, more like a sea anemone – those strange flowers you see in aquariums – than the pink thing Mama keeps hidden among her underwear. I wonder if, as I grow up, it will become more like the pink thing, and would it make the same noise, or maybe just a faint hissing like it is now with the bath foam sizzling around it?

I've been in the bath long enough now, my fingers are wrinkled.

'Come on, get out of the water. Can't you see that your fingers are all wrinkled? How many times do I have to tell you?'

'I told you, dear, raising a boy is war.'

Grandma would stand ready with the towel with blue-and-white anchors on it, a ham sandwich and some apricots that have been in the sun so long they're almost rotten.

Grandma would always talk too loud because she's a bit deaf, especially in the right ear, which is enormous and sawn in two by a dangly earring that's too heavy, and Mama would plead: 'Please, don't talk like that in front of the child.'

I pull out the plug. When the water has finished going down, the drain burps, telling us that's that, I'm all done digesting: foam, pieces of skin, black bits from my feet, a little fart. I put on Mama's dressing gown like a boxer in a daze at the end of the first round and, since I'm here, I brush my teeth. Not all of them though; just the front ones. In the mirror you can't see 'fucking shit' any more, just my face, and it's hard to read what was written there. I make faces. I yawn, like a hippopotamus from the documentaries. I'm sleepy.

Where's my duvet with the baby-blue clouds?

First I have to go and say hi to Mama.

I don't really want to.

I'd prefer not to see her, and instead remember her more alive than dead, like film stars. When they die the images we get shown are how they were when they were alive, not when they're all pale and wasted. That way you're happier to remember them.

The most they give us are pictures of the smashed-up cars, if they died in a car crash, like Princess Diana, who in my opinion was a lot less pretty than Mama.

The only picture I've got in my head of the famous

vanishing dad is of him and Mama smiling in front of a motorcycle, him with a red bandana round his neck and her in a leather jacket, her long hair blown all over to one side by the wind. Behind them there's a house like a hotel, I think, though I wouldn't swear to it, because at a certain point Mama stopped showing me that picture.

'I lost it. I can't find it any more.'

So I stand dawdling at the door, leaning against the door frame, dripping bath water onto the floor, unsure whether to go in or not. I turn round and fall asleep on the sofa. I like sleeping on the sofa even if I have the painting with the yucky weather above my head. I'm a little scared about having nightmares again, but then I fall into a dreamless sleep, my koala on the pillow and Blue tucked up close.

5

Saturday, which is just as well.

School finishes early.

Mama says she doesn't understand why children have to go to school on Saturdays, when their parents aren't working. I don't see why that matters to her, seeing as how she never goes anywhere anyway.

'That has nothing to do with it. It's about sleep. At least on Saturday people can sleep in.'

She's right, even if now it's not a problem any more.

My problem is finding my shoes with the laces, because the ones I wore yesterday are sure to sound like they have frogs in them still. Everything is in the storage closet: Mama's fancy high heels that she never wears any more, riding boots, even though we only went horse-riding once, even swimming flippers, but not what I'm looking for.

You pay attention to details and then go to school wearing flippers in the middle of winter. Not such a clever idea.

I put on yesterday's shoes, even though they're

soaking wet. When I walk in them they go croak, croak, or maybe it's more like the sound of kneading pizza dough. But when you walk in fresh snow the noise is just like when you crack meringue with a spoon. When I was little I thought snow was made by ghosts.

At least it's stopped raining today.

To make up for it it's colder again.

I keep my pyjamas on underneath my clothes, because they keep me warm and because it's quicker that way. And anyway at Saturday school nobody cares about anything, because it's Saturday. Everyone lets things go, already thinking about something else.

Davide and his parents are going to the mountains, because if it's rained this much here in the city there'll be loads of snow in the mountains.

Chubby Broccolo's going to stay with his relatives in Puglia for one of their birthdays. They'll eat heaps of orecchiette pasta with broccoli. I don't know what Antonella's doing, but she seems like the type who always knows what to do. The others . . . I have no idea.

Luca's spending the weekend at home with his mother, for all I know.

I've always hated it when they make you write about the weekend for your homework, or 'What did you do on your holiday?' They do it to find out about your business and then use what they find out against you as soon as you mess up.

So I write a story about the adventures of Blue, who's a cat who seems like a cartoon. That way everyone has fun, including me.

Blue's ears are always cold, so I explain how when he was made, after they'd given him whiskers, a tail, little heart-shaped pads under his feet and everything else, they realised they'd run out of ears. They had to attach ones they took straight from the freezer, but first they made a mistake and attached two orecchiette with broccoli, so he miaowed in Pugliese like Chubby in the third row, and no one understood what he was miaowing about. Then thanks to Chubby's translation they replaced the pasta with proper cat ears and solved the problem. We clink our glasses and say 'cheers!' to celebrate and Chubby gets an 'Excellent' on his classwork.

Making it up as I go along, and smiling, I get by.

Even better than poor Chubby Broccolo from Brindisi does, actually.

One time before we had Blue I told a story about seeing a gigantic mosquito on the wall of the kitchen next to the refrigerator. It was huge, with such long skinny legs that it seemed harmless. But everyone was so worried about the malaria the Africans were bringing into the city they didn't bother with the details of my private life.

Our science teacher talked to us about diseases in the Developing World.

'It's not the Africans' fault if they bring diseases here, because it's not their fault if they're sick. It's because they're poor.'

'Why do mosquitos only sting poor people?'

'Maybe poor people are tastier?'

'Why?'

As we leave we all say goodbye. I wave. 'Ciao, ciao.'

I've just gone through the main door when I hear Mrs Squarzetti calling me back.

'Luca! Luca!'

Suddenly I'm terrified again. Where did I mess up?

'Sorry, Luca, but your mother forgot this last time we saw each other. Would you be so kind as to give it to her?'

She hands me my progress report and gives me a smile, showing off a mouthful of crooked teeth, then turns – hurry-hurry – on her heel. It's Saturday for her too.

This is what the authorities have to say about Luca:

> Luca displays self-confidence and a lively disposition.
>
> He is endowed with considerable intelligence and

> a sense of responsibility. The pupil succeeds in all subjects. He consistently applies himself and the results are excellent. He has demonstrated a good deal of interest and ability in artistic activities and a notable interest in science and history. Kind-hearted and generous, he does all he can for his classmates and is full of initiative.

The pupil Luca responds: 'Go fuck yourselves, every last one of you.'

Arsefaces. What do you know about being full of initiative, kind-hearted and generous? The only generous part of you is your arsehole, the source of all your bullshit.

I don't know why but I'm so furious.

Well, I know why, but that just makes me twice as furious. For the first time in days there's a blue streak in the sky that you can pick out between the raggedy clouds at the end of the street, but I don't even know what to make of it.

I march home with the report in my hand and the wind in my face, feeling more and more desperate with every step to shut the door behind me soon, sooner, soonest, as soon as soon can be.

The perfect image of a mama, the perfect image of

a beautiful child, the perfect picture of health! Too bad Mama can't read it and Dad disappeared into smoke and I've got a fucking shit of a weekend ahead of me. Too bad that not long from now Mama's going to start to really stink.

Corpses stink after a bit, regardless of your sense of responsibility. It's a chemical process that can't be stopped. Even Lieutenant Columbo says so. After three days corpses stink, just like fish and house guests, but getting rid of it is not so simple, even if you're bursting with initiative. I can't send Mama to a hotel or off to stink out some other relative's place.

You think someone's dead then and there, but it's not true.

If I tell you Mama's stone dead in her bed, my artistic gifts will no longer be of interest to you; you'll send me straight to an orphanage to throw up little pasta tubes.

My eyes fill up with hot water again. Fucking shit, I'm in the shitty fucking shit.

And I have an entire weekend ahead of me.

It's strange. As I'm thinking all these things I realise I'm already inside the flat, leaning back against the front door to catch my breath, the little swinging cover over the spyhole winking at the lift.

It's strange but I feel safer here inside the flat, even with my dead mama's body in the bed, than out there.

It seems less serious. Here, inside, no one can hurt us. Here, inside, no one can come and pull me out just to put me in some other place I'll never get out of, where no one will care about me, because they're paid to care, which doesn't count. It's all a cheat. Like Grandma playing solitaire, when she chooses her cards and then boasts about always winning. I'm not falling for it. I try to turn the key again but it's already turned as far as it can go. I sneeze hard two or three times.

Even if my hideout isn't much, even if here on the eighth floor it feels like living on stilts, like those shacks where all it takes is one gust of wind from the north to knock them down, it's still a home. Like the 'Unsafe Building' in the piazza out front, which has had a sign saying that since before we moved in and nothing's changed. In any case the building is still there, and sometimes homeless guys sleep inside. Since they don't usually have a roof over their heads they make do with one that might fall in at any moment. I'm sure even homeless guys would say, 'Better here than in a homeless shelter.'

I go to Mama and read her the progress report.

For the first time since she stopped getting up I lie down next to her.

With my weight I pin down one of her arms under the covers.

I stretch out at her side as if we have all kinds of time ahead of us. An entire weekend. As if we have all the time in the world just to lie here side by side. As if my time was the same as hers.

I know that she's probably not interested in other people's progress any more, but then I'm not interested in her being dead either, in the strange blotches on her face, in how even with my stuffed-up nose I think I can tell she's started to smell. If everything wasn't becoming so complicated I'd say it's all the same to me, that in some ways I understand her, that I understand if she was sick of living.

It's just that maybe together we could have made it, if only she'd realised I was here, not just for changing the cat litter or growing up or causing problems. I should have told her that more often. And she could have made me understand more of what it was that really wasn't going right. We had a deal. I don't know if it was her or me who broke it.

Across from the bed there's a dresser and on top of the dresser there are pictures of us in silver frames: me in a swing, Grandma looking like the Madonna of Loreto, Mama after graduating from university and looking like she'd showed up at the wrong party, a photo of Blue taken the day he came to live with us. Mama's dresser used to be Grandma's. We only put the nicest pictures up there, with all the arsefaces cut out because they'd spoil the scene.

I look at Mama and think, All in all she's a lot better than Davide's mama. Even now when she's so different.

I look on top of the dresser for the plastic bag with her make-up. It has to be here, even if she doesn't use it much.

I find lipstick and a tin shaped like a clam shell. I think it's face powder. Inside it's pink and cracked like a lump of desert, with a little sponge on top.

I come up close to Mama and try to put some lipstick on her. It's not easy to follow the outline of her lips; the red gets into the wrinkles round her puckered mouth and smudges everywhere. I'm making a mess. I try to make it better with the sponge, adding some colour to her swollen cheeks. I don't know if she's happy, but maybe she is.

She looks a little ridiculous, made up like that.

'My beautiful, celestial rose,' Grandma would say to her, as she was always saying everything and just the opposite of everything.

I stretch out again and try to think about how it was before.

I close my eyes, trying to remember how it was when she had her make-up done properly, with her hair combed and she's dressed up. Inside my eyes I can see the little silver rectangles of the photo frames. Inside the photos I can see her, elegant, all dressed in white, with baby me in her arms. I'm wrapped up in a blanket embroidered with little pink flowers . . . were they pink or blue? Pink, yes, they were definitely pink. Maybe Mama thought I'd be a girl?

'I told you, dear, raising a boy is war.'

'Please, don't talk like that in front of the child.'

I suck on the soft, warm blanket, made for someone else, like it was her tit. I almost suffocate on a wool thread that gets in my throat, goes up my nose, puts down poisonous roots that intertwine with my veins. They grow and make me explode from inside, like the trees that break through the street. Once again I'm in the hospital; again the nurses steal my biscuits. We're back at the beginning, like in the Game of the Goose we play at New Year's.

The goose that the flower woman ate for Christmas.

I wake up screaming. There's a dead body next to me! I scream louder. No one can hear me.

Everyone's away for the weekend.

'Upsy-daisy, up-up-upsy-daisy!'

Me again, teeny-tiny, tossed up in the air, trapped in a girl's blanket; the chandelier with the crystal beads coming closer and closer; me terrified they're not able to hold me tight enough. Please take pity on me, please put me down.

'Upsy-daisy, how wonderful it is to fly through the sky!'

I'm scared, so scared.

I scream. I scream like in a horror film, scream as if all the bumps I'd ever avoided, all the times I didn't fall, the times I survived, as if they happed all at once. I scream as if I was nothing but a scream.

The scream becomes hard like a stalagmite in the frozen cave of Mama's room.

I run out and swear I'll never go back in, never again.

I run into the bathroom to wash my face and hands.

Fear is all I feel. Again I have trouble breathing. I curl up on the armchair in the living room. I feel like I need to pee. I should get up and go back to the bathroom but instead I stay huddled in the chair.

I don't want to cross the hall any more. The hall is the Grand Canyon, a swamp infested with crocodiles crying pointlessly.

My reservoir of tears is dry again but plenty of

pee is leaking out. At first I try to hold it. Then I can't take it any more. I feel hot liquid running down my legs, but at the same time I feel heat rising and rising through the rest of my body, so then I try to get the pee out more quickly. I squeeze and squeeze, wringing myself out like a dishcloth. The chair is stained all over. I know I shouldn't do it but I like doing it. The circle of pee gets bigger on the yellow velvet that goes all dark brown. I learn how great it is to piss like this.

Blue comes over. I blow in his face and he runs away.

I'm exhausted but I'd like to piss some more.

From now on I want to piss everywhere, like a cat in heat. I'd like to be Blue and piss wherever I feel like it. I'd like to piss piss piss and never stop pissing. On door frames, on chair legs, on tram seats next to old ladies with their shopping bags between their legs and celery stalks for their soup sticking out like surprise bursts of nature. I'd like to piss on my desk at school and hear the rain of piss drip down onto the lino floor, drip drip drip, like in some romantic poem. I'd like to piss on the heads of the parents (or legal guardians) on the last line of the progress report, and blot out the comments from those people who can't judge me because they don't really know me, like when I spit out 'Paris' with lots of 'P's on my notebook. I'd like to piss on the lives of strangers who think they know everything and don't know anything, and on my own life that maybe will never see Paris.

I'm worn out.

I'd like to piss again.

But I can't.

I've got nothing left inside.

The pee reservoir is empty now too.

I'm full of emptiness.

It's only three in the afternoon.

Still in the chair I look at the stain, which has got bigger and now looks like a blank map, like the ones where you've got to fill in the names of the countries, the cities, the mountains and the lakes, but you can't do it because you can't figure out where in the world it is. My trousers are warm and wet and sticking to my legs. I try to think how everything will be when it's all over, even if it's just begun.

I don't know.

All I know is that I don't want to end up in an orphanage.

I want to stay in this house, which is beautiful even if I don't like Grandma's furniture. I don't want to have a tiny metal wardrobe to put my stuff in and I don't want fluorescent lights that make everyone pale like at the morgue, and I don't want to have to ask permission for every little thing and I don't want to drink raw eggs every morning like the nuns made me do, and I don't want grey blankets and grey everything. I don't want to be afraid to stretch out my legs to the far end of the bed, don't want icy cold sheets, don't want to be frozen with my armpits sweating cold sweat and penguin guano between my thighs because at the far end of the bed, at the very place where feet turn into stumps gnawed on by ghosts, there's the Antarctic. I don't want to slip down into the glaciers, where the cold bites your ankles. I want to stay here. I don't want to fall into the third, fourth, fifth world, all the way to the last page of the atlas. Into the third, fourth, last world where they sell children, or sell their spare parts. At the edge of the world there's nothing but seals and penguins, and sea lions that eat their own pups.

And, more than anything else, I don't want to live without my incredible cat Blue. In orphanages they bring you cat for dinner, passing it off as stewed rabbit.

Blue jumps into my arms, as if he could read my thoughts, even though thinking about afterwards, now, is very difficult. Right now there's nothing but a big now that grows and looks like a blank map.

At most I can think about *after* afterwards, which is

much later in time. I can imagine how it will be when I'm a vet and taking care of cats that piss everywhere.

I can dream about getting engaged to Antonella, and about marrying her and making her belly grow with a baby inside.

About returning home and telling her how I treated an armadillo or a capybara, collectible card number fifty-five, the one that's always missing.

About how I saved some very rare animals, including a sloth, the one that moves in slow motion like Mama, number seventy-eight.

About Antonella saying to me, '*Amore*, with those glasses you look like a bespectacled bear.'

Because it's likely that when I grow up I'll wear glasses.

The kind that magnify details.

Some detail must have escaped me about Mama. Maybe there was something that should have made me understand that she wouldn't be waking up any more. But even when I try hard to remember every detail, it seems like she was the same as usual, the other night. Not worse than usual.

For dinner we had chicken thighs and potatoes, and she ate them too. She took two, leaving me the ones with the crispy skin. Blue jumped up on the table and tried to snatch a piece of chicken with his paw, and Mama said, 'Don't give the bones to Blue because little chicken bones can puncture a cat's stomach.'

'Mama, why is Blue always hungry?'

She didn't reply. She never does when I ask pointless questions. I just want to get a conversation started. I understand when now's not the time but every once in a while I keep trying. If I play the fool a little bit, I say to myself, maybe she'll have fun. If I make her laugh maybe the sadness will go away.

The other night we must not have talked much because I remember the buzz of the refrigerator and the sound of the forks being laid down on the plates and the scrape, scrape of her fingernail as she scratched the label on the mineral water bottle. But it's often like that, that Mama doesn't talk much. Mama's never a chatterbox.

Actually, sometimes when she speaks she doesn't even finish her sentences, as if the words won't come to her, and I tell her, 'Careful or flies will fly in,' because she says it to me too if I sit there with my mouth open.

'Don't sit there with your mouth open. You look like an imbecile.'

And it's not obvious that when someone is sad it's a mistake to take medicine. Or that when someone is sad and it *is* a mistake to take medicine, the medicine will make that person never wake up again.

Mistakes happen.

Once I made a mistake, putting a bean up my nose while Mama was chopping vegetables for the minestrone. To be honest I had done it a bit on purpose, because I wanted to see how far up it could go, but I was also bored sitting there watching her being so focused on cooking, with no thought of paying any attention to me.

I realised I'd made a mistake because the bean wouldn't come down any more and I could only breathe out of half of my nose. Mama tried to help me, shaking her head with a look on her face that was half worried and half depressed.

'Do I really have to deal with a son like this, worse than his own . . .'

'My own what?'

'Worse than everybody, worse than nobody, let's just drop it, so long as you don't get the idea to stick beans up your nose again.'

So after that I was more careful.

When I looked in her drawers, that was a mistake too. But what does that even mean? Every once in a while you can make a mistake, nobody dies.

This is all not right.

It's not right.

Not right not right not right.

The soaking-wet bits of my trousers are all cold, like an ice pack you put on bruises. I drag myself to my room and put on tracksuit trousers. Before I put them on I dry the dampness left between my legs with my dirty Power Rangers T-shirt.

I leave everything on the floor. Who's going to tell me to clean it up?

I'm the master of the house and Blue is top cat, my personal assistant.

'Assistant! To the remote controls! The master of the house wishes to watch TV.'

'Remote controls ready.'

'Ready, *sir*. You have to say "sir".'

'Ready, sir.'

'Tail straight?'

'Completely straight!'

'Very well, Blue. It's good that you're here.'

'Affirmative, sir.'

'T-minus and counting: three, two, one!'

Blue and I dive into the cosmic universe. We float like heavenly bodies, him Blue and me celestial blue, in the stratosphere of the sofa.

'Blue, what are your antennae picking up?'

'Exploding white dwarf stars, sir.'

'Like popcorn?'

'Yes, sir, very much like popcorn.'

'Well done, Blue, I knew I could count on you. Initiate Mission Popcorn. Cross Hallway Galaxy, reach Planet Kitchen. Prepare to land, assistant, touch down!'

I set Blue down on the table and he seems more terrified than terra-firmed. He doesn't like it so much when I make him fly through outer space, but he lets me do it, mostly because he hopes to get something to eat.

'Upsy-daisy, up-up-upsy-daisy! Not so great, eh, being at the mercy of human beings?'

There's still half a packet of popcorn left. They're a bit squishy because it's rained so much.

Doesn't matter.

'Mission accomplished, assistant. Return immediately to the stratosphere.'

Blue tries to run away but I catch him. On the sofa again he purrs and spits popcorn everywhere.

Blue is an omnivore, like a bear. Sometimes he ruminates, with his omasum and abomasum, like sheep. Sometimes he squeaks, like a squirrel. If you pay attention a cat is many things besides a cat.

The day we got him, on my birthday, he looked like a mouse more than anything else. He was mangy and you could hold him in the palm of a hand.

The first few days he holed up under the bed. I shut myself up in the wardrobe out of spite. Mama shut herself up in herself.

Then Blue got used to us and we to him.

Soon it will be Mama's birthday.

Question: When people are dead do they still have birthdays, or do they stop?

Mama will be thirty-seven years old. I'll bring her a bunch of flowers – flowers are good whether you're alive or dead.

Mama is a Pisces. Like a fish she lives on the other side of a sheet of glass that separates her from the rest of the world. Sometimes she makes an effort: she leaps from the other side and then she's a fish out of water. You can see right away she's not comfortable.

'Horoscopes are all nonsense.'

She always reads them though, as if in her heart she really does hope to find something true in there: love, health, money, a new job.

'You're lucky to be a Gemini, the Twins, because Geminis are friendly and cheerful. Whereas Pisces have a melancholy nature, and are a bit introverted.'

In the movies the spaceship floats in the sky, the astronauts are suspended upside down, and the stars trace horoscopes in reverse, like ours – mine and Mama's – where what happens is always the opposite of what's supposed to happen.

The astronauts move their mouths like fish. They speak but seem like they're mute because they're so far away no one can hear them. They eat coloured pills that they keep in the spaceship cabinet, instead of the bathroom cabinet.

Blue is still hungry. We're out of cat biscuits and he ate the last tin of food this morning. I really don't know what to give him to eat. I have to go out. Blue starts to chase my shoelaces, gets between my feet while I'm putting on my jacket, follows me all the way to the door.

'Wait for me here. I'll be right back. Don't worry.'

I check the coins in my pockets and find only five twos, three ones, and four fifty-cent pieces. Like playing battleships.

How long can the money last?

In the little shop round the corner I buy a discount package of beef and two packets of crisps. I walk round the block to get a bit of air, pass by the newsagent but don't stop. I don't have enough money for what's not useful.

When I open the door to our flat an unbelievable stench hits me right in the face. It must be Mama.

With a scarf over my mouth I walk towards her room, and the stink becomes stronger. It's Mama who stinks – stinks like a corpse.

I drop the bag and, holding my breath, rush to the end of the hallway. I run to her window and try to turn the handle. It sticks, but with both hands I throw it wide open, and the curtains fly against my face like spirits trying to take me away. And I feel possessed as I turn round, trip over a shoe, and almost fall, and reach the bedroom door. I feel like I'm going to explode. I close Mama and her horrible stink in her room and turn the key. I'm out of breath.

But now I have to run and open all the other windows too, all of them, as fast as I can. I feel like breathing so much, I can't. Finally I fill my lungs with just the air from the balcony, letting in the cold that cuts the smell like a knife.

The stink stays stuck to me everywhere. I smell nothing but stink inside my nose, all the way down inside my belly. I sniff my hands – they stink. Everything stinks.

Blue circles round me, eyes wide.

'What's the matter? Why are you opening all these windows in the middle of winter? Why are you all behaving so strangely? Why can't we all just curl up happily next to the heater?'

He tries to lick me, his way of kissing me, but I push him away.

It seems to me he doesn't have his delicate stuffed-animal smell any more, just an awful pong.

I see him and then I don't. The whole room is spinning around me. I hear a buzzing in my head, the refrigerator noise but louder, the noise of the pink thing that Mama hides in her drawer but a thousand times louder. So, so loud and then, suddenly, not at all.

Maybe I passed out. I've never passed out before but I imagine this is what it is like. Everything spins and you fall on the floor.

As if someone threw a heavy coat on top of you.

As if you were dead.

But you're not dead.

If I touch myself I feel it. I'm not sure how long I stayed on the floor but I'm fairly sure I'm still alive.

Maybe I just fell asleep, like Blue when you put the lead on him.

The coat, I remember, is missing its sleeves, but I can still breathe through two stumps.

Or else I'm really dead. Maybe that's how dead people feel; everything is the same as before except they can no longer change anything. They see everything going wrong but they can't do anything any more.

If I'm dead, sooner or later I'll start to smell like Mama. It's so cold. The smell now seems less strong. The French doors are open, as if we're in the middle of summer.

I try to slap myself but I don't know how hard to do it.

It's not easy to slap yourself, on your own.

'Take back what you said.'

'No.'

'Take it back right now.'

'No, no, and for the last time, no.'

Pow! The slap stuck to my cheek for a while, like a nasty hot stink. I spent the afternoon in the wardrobe, thinking I'd never, ever leave.

The stink.

I knew that it would come sooner or later, and maybe it was there before too, just not as strong. Or maybe it's because I went outside that it seemed more disgusting, like when every day you grow a little and you don't realise it, but if someone you haven't seen for a while runs into you on the street, he says, 'How you've grown!'

It's true, that's how it is. The things that grow slowly always seem the same if you live there; if you see them from outside they're different.

I never want to go into Mama's room again.

I hope the cold freezes her, like the mummy they found in the glaciers. I dig about in my head to find something to compare this to, but it's not there. I hope that no worms come, like with zombies.

Grandpa used to fish with worms.

'Just look at my lovable larvae,' he would say, opening a plastic Tupperware, the kind used for keeping leftovers in the refrigerator.

'You see these ones? These are the Kennedy maggots. And these? Pope John. These other ones are my Marilyn maggots.'

The worms of famous people who died in his day, that's how he classified them. The biggest ones got the most important names. He was very proud of his worms.

I don't want to think about worms.

I don't want to think about anything any more.

I have to learn how not to think.

There must be a system.

If you don't want to listen all you have to do is put

your fingers in your ears and sing loudly. What can you do in order not to think?

My head is filled with ideas, stupid and not stupid; it does everything on its own. I can't control it. There's no switch to turn off the maggots moving in my head and then coming out of my eyes, the brain with its wormy white spirals, like Grandpa's maggots moving in the cranial container, hidden on a shelf in the storage closet instead of the kitchen.

The TV stares at me with its giant shiny pupil like some Jurassic animal. I see my reflection in it. I'd like to be sucked through the screen to the other side, into the body of the television, like Alice. Everything goes marvellously well for the kids inside the screen. Even if a story starts out and things are only so-so, then comes the happy ending: the adults make up, everyone's problems disappear, dogs wag their tails and slobber all over your face. It's true that the TV news only shows sad stories, but that's because they take the pictures from reality, things that really happened. Once they're sucked into the TV though, they seem less real, that is they seem real but fake at the same time. You're sorry, but not all that much, and mostly you just forget it right away.

Why doesn't it work with me?

I never behaved that badly, and still I couldn't convince anyone to make things happen differently. Not even Mama took the trouble to live for me. Why?

What do the others have that I haven't?

I've holed up under the duvet, just like in an earthquake on TV, even though the ceiling is still there and the walls are there and even the furniture, and the whole building is still standing. Even though everything is in its place: the sofa with me on top, the table shiny with wax, the chest of drawers with the mirror, the piss-stained armchair, the painting full of yucky weather signed by one of the cat's ancestors.

The house seems naked. I feel like I should whisper, like in a museum, even though I don't know who to talk to.

If people saw me on TV like this, a pig in a blanket, I'm sure their hearts would break: poor kid, what a beautiful child, look what's been done to him, my heart breaks just to see him. If instead they saw me in the flesh, alive and kicking and not decrepit at all, I'm sure they'd send me straight to an orphanage, as soon as they'd finished exhausting me with questions to work out how disturbed I am, because they'd never believe me. They'd never believe someone would stay with his dead mother in the house because he doesn't want to go to an orphanage. It's too simple an explanation, so of course they'd have to look for other ones.

Saying that I don't want to abandon Blue would never be enough.

And yet sometimes the dogs that people abandon at motorway services travel miles and miles to return home. They show up at the door as if to say, 'Here I am!'

Because dogs don't want to end up in kennels, either.

Better to go back to their owners, even if they're bastards.

I don't know what I'll do.

But maybe I'll get an idea.

Nobody pays much attention to us anyway. Maybe that's how things will stay.

I go and pick up the shopping bag I left in the hallway. I put the tins of food away. I rinse Blue's bowl and put a little food inside. I cover the open tin with foil and put it in the fridge.

At the same time I decide to start a new life.

You can't put groceries away and decide your future. You can't do two things at once.

And yet now I can; I can do everything.

So I decide to do the same things I did with Mama, just without her. It can't be impossible.

I tell myself: it's just as if you've grown up.

All of a sudden.

I'm your typical single guy and I'm stuck at home because it's very much winter outside. I just have to keep to myself. I have to make it work.

How many times have I wanted to grow up soon, straight away? Here we go. It's happened. It might have happened better, but that's how it is. That's all.

What do adults on their own do when they're home alone?

All I can do is imagine and copy.

I imagine that single people read the newspaper. Fine. That's what I'll do.

I pick up a magazine and read it. I like reading, why shouldn't I do it now? Mama's newspaper has an article that says that single people make up 25 per cent of our country's population. Fine. Now there's one more.

I'm not an orphan. I'm single.

It's just a matter of words. Sometimes words can even change ideas and points of view. In order to be an adult, fuck, all you've got to do to is use adult words. Like a driving licence: you've got to be a certain age to express yourself in a certain way – before you can't. And yet there's no exam to test your ability to drive words in the right direction.

I can say all the dirty words I want, I can jump red lights now that I'm alone. I can also blaspheme, use the dirtiest dirty words of them all, because God hasn't woken up Mama, and so he deserves it. I just have to make sure nobody hears me.

I have a go at God: 'Fuck you, God.'

I have trouble at first, like when I have to stick out my tongue as far as I can to see if I've got spots on my tonsils, but then I manage.

It's not that fun, but I said it.

'Fuck you, God. God, Fuck you.'

I could light up a cigarette, too, if I wanted, and smoke it at the window looking out at the smoking chimneys on the rooftops, like Mama, who looks out and the smoke seems to come out of her head, because her thoughts are burning up.

Mama's cigarettes are right here, on the table, and also the lighter with the word 'Love' on it, inviting me to become big right away.

I wonder if single people are happy to be single.

Whether they don't miss the goodnight kiss, and that face-cream smell that stays a while on your cheek and on your pillow too – Mama's protective cream, which fights wrinkles and also bad dreams.

The good thing is that I don't have to eat tonight, or wash, or force myself to be cheerful, not tonight.

Tomorrow is Sunday, everyone's day off.

I wear myself out with comics; I've read almost all of them before. I crunch on biscuits. There's a surprise in the packet, a toy clown who runs in zigzags on just one wheel.

With biscuit crumbs inside the duvet, on the sofa, between my teeth, I try to sleep. I dream about losing all my teeth, one by one. My teeth begin to wobble, then they slip out easily, without pain, without screams. The gums are left empty, like when you pull petals off daisies to play She loves me, she loves me not. I don't know how I'll be able to go to school without teeth. I don't know what I'll do if I can't smile any more.

6

Today's Sunday. No school.

It seems a lot like yesterday, and yet, school or no school it's today. The sun is out though. It's weak but I can see it through a pane in the French door. I spot it curled up in the light-blue clouds, with Blue beside me and my finger running over the sharp ridges of teeth that seem like mountain ranges inside my mouth.

Single people get up late on Sundays because they don't have anything to do, so I turn over and keep sleeping.

This time I dream about my friend Davide. We're riding bikes along a promenade. Then a man shows up and says that bikes aren't allowed on the promenade, so we pedal harder, because if we pedal fast enough we might lift off. Davide breaks away from earth first and begins to flutter like a butterfly. His mama sees us from far away and moves her arms like she's swatting flies.

'Come here, come here before you hurt yourself. You'll burn if you stay out in the sun too long.'

I pedal lots and lots but stay lower down. In my

dream I dream of soaring up into the sky and turning in circles on my outstretched wings with the seagulls, above all the houses and everything. I dream of seeing the sea look small like the sparkly piece of mirror that's the pond in the nativity scene, but I pedal like crazy and only seem like a bee, which moves super fast just to stay in place in the air. Then my legs can't take it any more: I get a cramp in one of my calf muscles. I come close to falling, maybe I do fall. I fall but don't touch the bottom. I wake up first.

I wake up again with Blue asleep on my right leg that's fallen asleep. If I touch it it's like it's someone else's leg, like they've put it in my bed in order to play another nasty trick on me.

I'd like to keep sleeping but I'm not sleepy any more.

I drag myself to the bathroom and sit down to pee like a girl. Mama says it's better that way because I don't leave drips on the seat, and to be honest it's also comfortable. I can stay on the toilet as long as I want, without even having to poo on command.

Today being Sunday I'd like to celebrate and not take a poo and invent something new, but even if everything's new nothing original comes to mind. The only wants that come to me are old ones, used a million times, worn out and faded by the tumble dryer of everything that's happened.

I would really like to go on a bike ride like I did when we used to visit Grandma, before she lost her marbles and they carried her off to Villa Serena.

'Mama, why don't we go to Grandma's any more?'

'Because she's not doing so well.'

Grandma lost her marbles or, as we say, lost the *tramontana* – or maybe she gained it: the wind got into her brain and tangled up all her ideas.

'Does the wind do that?'

'Yes, sometimes the wind can drive people crazy.'

The only things that come into my head are ideas so normal it's crazy not to be able to make them happen. But maybe I couldn't have even before, because Mama was tired and never wanted to do anything. For me nostalgia is only nostalgia for an idea, even if then nostalgia catches me in the stomach and it feels like hunger pains.

Mama likes to spend hours looking out of the window and it's clear that, for her, outside is very far away. She's looking out of the window of an aeroplane, not our house.

Not all that much has changed.

Sometimes, sure, if I really insist Mama goes along

with my ideas, but it's one thing to have someone doing things she doesn't want to, just to make you happy, and totally another if someone is actually having fun.

Now I'm a coat that's missing both sleeves.

When we'd go to the seaside to visit Grandma, who lived in a city with the sea right in the city, I could ride my bike everyday. I'd slalom between the people in swimsuits, in the street too. Then we'd stop to have a chocolate and pistachio gelato, and sit in the sun, and make fun of the chubby girls in the water with their lifebelts of chub round their bellies. We'd go back to Grandma's house at lunchtime, and when I stepped into the house, for a minute it was like I'd gone blind, because outside there was so much light and inside it was so dark. The first time I was frightened and really thought I had gone blind, like one of those guys with the German shepherds and white sticks and a pimply alphabet they have to feel on the pages. I burst out crying, until little by little my eyes became used to the dark and I stopped crying and being afraid.

I also liked to lick the salt on my smooth tanned skin, like Blue when he smooths down his fur. I liked the smell of salt and the fact that by scratching the dry salt with my fingernail I could make doodles and tattoos on my skin like Indian chiefs have. Then I'd have to take a shower, but I'd try to save at least an arm, so I could lick it at night too, under the heavy cotton sheets that smelled new even if they were the same ancient sheets from Grandma's trousseau.

They'd say, 'You're not a goat. Goats like salt.'

Or: 'You're a goat, because you're ignorant.'

But they didn't really think that. They just said it to make fun of me.

Cities by the sea are more beautiful because they're half city and half sea. I live in an all-city city, and that's what they call the street map. If you get lost you can always check the all-city map, the *Tuttocittà*, even if you can't take your bike and go to the sea.

In the city we live in everything is city.

I don't know what to do about this for now.

I'm forced to invent something else.

So I invent.

There's a rotting corpse in my bed, so I teleport it to the emergency room. The forensics expert confirms that its anatomical-functional capacities are damaged beyond repair and says it's a fine mess. The vet however, who's secretly in love with Mama, doesn't want to give up, so he asks himself if there's not something he can do for her. The vet consults with lots and lots of doctors from all over the world and each one offers his own opinion about how to solve the problem. One says there are ghosts capable of bringing corpses back to life, that Mama can be reanimated if we find the right ghost or some good ectoplasm. In that case Mama could live with me, but only in the evenings and at night. Another says it's possible to resuscitate at least a part of Mama, the part where she's my mama and not just any person. Yet another says we could create an android Mama, a kind of babysitter that's a bit stupid but who can do the job. A doctor from Egypt says we need to call a certain scientist who knows how to mammify mamas, to wrap them in bandages in such a way that mamas stay mamas even when they die, and wake back up when it's really necessary. I tell him I'm trying to freeze Mama, to preserve her for as long as possible, while we wait for someone to invent some coloured pills that, if you take lots and lots, will make you live instead of die. The vet says that's a good idea, that he'll start studying it, that we'll find a way.

Then the vet takes me out for pizza. Looking at me with his big eyes, made bigger by his glasses, he tells me I shouldn't worry, that he'll take care of it. On a Sunday the restaurant is full of people: there are couples, families – and us. I like that they see me with the vet, also the fact that he's a doctor, not that people know but it's easy to tell. He's nice to the waiters too, who are going crazy because it's Sunday and everyone is so hungry it's like they haven't eaten for a week. I try to cut my pizza with a knife and fork because I don't feel like eating it with my hands. I want to show I have good manners like him. We talk a lot, not just about Mama, and it's not like meeting with the school doctors who want to dig into your business just to keep you under their thumb. He asks me about stuff like it really matters to him, then he pretends what I tell him isn't a big deal. That's what he does when we take Blue to him too. I know it's not his cat, but he treats him as if he was; that's what I like about him. We also talk about lions. The vet explains to me how it's the lionesses who go out hunting and bring back food to their cubs. He also says the hunt is successful one out of every seven attempts, that sometimes it's hard for them too, even though they're such strong animals. He also tells me about how one time a group of lionesses adopted a gazelle instead of eating it, and it was an incredible event because nobody had ever seen anything like it between such different species. Even the newspapers wrote about it. He tells me that, if I want, until they find the medicine to wake up Mama, he could adopt me too, even if we belong to such different species. I'm happy because that way I won't end up in an orphanage, and Blue will have his own doctor all to himself. I imagine my new life with the vet who knows everything about animals. It seems so wonderful that I'm almost not sorry any more that Mama's frozen, and orphan-orphans just seem like poor creatures, a whole other category.

I'm wearing a white coat and standing next to him. I've got the sleeves rolled up because it's his coat. I'm helping him treat dogs and cats.

'Here we are, now hold him steady, carefully. Pet him softly and tell him how good he is. You'll see how he calms down.'

And that's how it is. When the vet talks with the cats the cats relax. The dogs accept the situation and become less scared.

At the end of office hours the patients go away wagging their tails, thanking us and smiling. We wash our hands, swiping the soap from each other, then we head to the laboratory to study and time passes and we don't even notice. We swap opinions like scientists do and pat each other on the back when we have a good idea. We're so smart, the smartest of them all. We'll figure it out for sure. Eventually we say goodbye to Mama who is hibernating in a special capsule made all of silver, behind a secret door in the laboratory, and we go home in Muddy Waters' jeep that's all dirty with mud from the savannah. When we open the door Blue comes up and greets us.

'Hi, guys, how are you?'

Because the vet is so smart he's also managed to teach Blue our language.

'Hey, what do you think, Blue? Wouldn't that be great?'

Blue stays quiet.

I look him straight in the eyes and he looks at me. His eyes are infinitely deep, like the Mariana Trench; nobody knows what's at the bottom.

Maybe Blue wouldn't like living with the vet. Maybe he hates him because the vet puts the thermometer up his bottom instead of under his arms or in his mouth like with human beings. Mama says there's no point in fantasising because there's nothing that's fantastic.

I eat some crisps, then I blow into the bag and burst it with a single blow, a gunshot. Blue is scared. He arches his back, leaps sideways and runs away. For the first time in my life I can't wait till it's Monday.

7

What an awful night.

As soon as I manage to fall truly asleep Blue begins to miaow like a madman. They sound more like howls than miaows, excruciating and never-ending, the miaowing of an animal being tortured. I get up to see what's going on, terrified by the thought that Blue feels unwell too.

I always sleep with the lights on now. At my house it's always bright and always cold, like the North Pole.

Bleary-eyed and dull-headed I drag myself into the hallway. I see Blue in front of the door to Mama's room. He wants to go in, he jumps up and bats the handle, jumps and miaows, scratches the door, desperate at not being able to open it. I pick him up and bring him back to the sofa. He doesn't want to stay. I have to squeeze him so hard I can feel his little bird's skeleton under his skin. As soon as I stop holding him he goes right back to the hallway. He starts to cry again and to jump like a monkey, with a determination you find only in the most ridiculously stubborn cats.

I have to get up early but can't sleep at all, I'm drowning in calm waters, flopping from one shore to the other. The duvet is all twisted up with my pyjamas, trapping me in an enormous straitjacket.

I'm the one who tells the alarm it's time to get up this morning.

'And you thought you were the only one who knew how, huh, arseface?'

At breakfast I explain to Blue that Mama's room is *off-limits*.

'*Off-limits*, *verboten*, *keine gegestande*, no *trippen* for *catten*.'

It's just like the little signs on the windows in trains; there's no point complaining so much.

I'm in a bad way, my face swollen into a good-little-boy mask that could sag and fall away at any moment, like a transfer that comes off in your fingers. I wash myself with both hands, letting the water slap me around. Back in my room I put on my trousers, sitting this time, search for two matching socks in the drawer, go through my jumpers. I put books and notebooks into my school-bag, go over in my mind all the operations I have to carry out, like the pilot preparing for take-off on the poster next to the window, the one with the tape all yellow and shrivelled.

I put my second life on over my coat and set off on a special mission.

I'm Dr Jekyll and Mr Hyde, a werewolf, Spiderman or Superduck, but my powers aren't so super. I don't scale walls. My fur hasn't grown yet. I don't transform into anything special. I dress up as a normal little boy, with combed hair and books that aren't dog-eared.

It's Monday morning, and the shops are still asleep. The town is having trouble leaving the night behind too. All the shutters, like eyelids, are still lowered over the shop windows. I walk slowly because I'm early, like old people who have insomnia and start shuffling around at dawn in order to live longer; like Grandma, who one day started talking to herself and reintroducing herself every time we saw each other.

'It's such a pleasure to meet you. I'm Ruggero's wife, and you're the captain's son, right?'

Grandma and her obsession with ships.

'Not just any ships, my dear, ocean liners.'

'Yes, Grandma, I know; the ones where the brass gleams like in church.'

'And where the polished floors are swept clean by evening gowns.'

'Yup, those are the ones.'

Always the same old enchanted cruise song.

'Who is this captain, Mama?'

'How should I know? Grandma's the one who invented all these stories. She's moved into an operetta and shut out everything else.'

She tells me to let it go, tapping her finger against her temple, trying not to be seen.

Even the flower woman's stall is shut up like an abandoned kennel. Maybe she's moved too. Or had an accident. It would serve her right.

When adults arrive early somewhere they stop in a café for an espresso. I buy myself a piece of focaccia, teeny-tiny to save money. There's a half-eaten strawberry sweet stuck to the two-euro coin, but luckily the lady behind the counter doesn't mind if the money is a bit sticky.

'If only money would always stick to my fingers.'

Along with the change she gives me a free lolly.

'How was your weekend?'

'Same old, same old.'

'You?'

I blah-blah-blah. My classmates' chattering bores me; they always say the same things. They're talking, but their voices seem to come from somewhere else, somewhere I used to live not too long ago myself. Now I've moved into a flat one floor up but I can't look down on them. I'd like to look the other way, but I can't; I must keep my head up and my tail straight. It's not so easy. It's like when you dream of being naked in the middle of a crowd of people fully dressed. You try to pretend it's nothing, but you know that you're naked, that you can't get dressed until the nightmare's over. I shiver in my coat.

In class they ask us what differentiates *Homo sapiens* from his ancestors.

'The ability to deceive,' I want to say. But I'm careful not to.

I get lost imagining my ancestors racking their brains to crack open a coconut, and then the ones who learn how to use weapons like bows and arrows, and they become more and more intelligent. They walk around naked, but so is everyone so nobody cares. Then someone makes the first coat out of animal fur, and it's especially the lady sapiens who want it. They call it a fur coat and wear it when they go shopping. They buy shoes that make them wobble and that get stuck in the grating over the Metro.

Mrs Squarzetti sapiens must have gone shopping last weekend too, because today she's got new shoes, shiny and black like cockroaches. She doesn't know how to drive them so well yet, because after a few steps she turns round and sits down again at her desk. The cockroach-shoes appear and disappear from view. I feel like crushing them with my exercise book.

Sooner or later cockroaches will overrun the planet, advancing on mountains of leftovers with shields shaped like dustbin lids, because cockroaches are resistant to poisons. They don't die just because of a handful of bad medicine.

They're the most intelligent of all, even if it doesn't take them seven months to be born.

Chubby Broccolo has fallen asleep at his desk, as he always does on Mondays, having arrived on the sleeper train from Puglia that reaches the station at dawn. The teachers all know, so they don't yell at him much. After all it's not his fault if he's got relatives so far away and he stinks like the train.

I'd like to sleep in a train berth myself. I'm also nodding off with sleep. I have relatives far away too.

When Mrs Squarzetti starts walking between the desks like someone unsure of the ground beneath her feet, I stop gazing at a damp spot that reminds me of a polar bear, or a crisp, or Lake Titicaca, and I smile – the secret is to do well in all your subjects and smile. Smiling is one of the responsibilities of a good ant who must do all he can to escape an endless number of Plagues of Egypt.

We're all ants, even if grasshoppers are much cooler.

'Do you know what happened in the end?' I murmur to Davide.

'The end of what?'

'The story of the ant and the grasshopper.'

'No, what?'

'The grasshopper who hadn't stored up any food for the winter, he ate the ant.'

'That's not the way it goes!'

'Who cares, Davide, the story's much better this way.'

I'm glad Davide is my friend.

8

I've run out of money.

Mama says money always runs out before you expect it. That's true. I should have remembered and planned for it. I should have looked for the secret code for the cash machine but I didn't. I didn't think of it. Now I've got to open that door one more time. The number must be in the document box in the bottom drawer. I don't want to but I must.

A missed detail has brought everything to a head: a wrecked car in the river, a non-biodegradable plastic bag caught in the rocks, a tramp's shoe, a moped set on fire at the end of a match by supporters of the other team.

In the last few days I've stopped being so afraid, as if my second life has begun to rub out my first, like a sheet of tissue paper making everything underneath look less clear, as if my life from before was bit by bit becoming a childhood memory, a thought that buzzes in your head but you can chase it away if you shake your arms.

Mama, on the other hand, is still in there.

I don't want to see her.

I don't want to smell the stink.

I don't have a choice.

I have to break the record for not breathing, I have to hold my breath with all the breath I have, hold it inside, suck myself in all the way to my arsehole.

I must turn away. I must hold out. I mustn't look.

I clench my fists so tightly that my knuckles go white, like boiled sweets all stuck together in a bag, joining forces to hold out against enemy attacks.

I have to go food shopping.

The supermarket is full of people.

I like trolleys full to bursting, the kind you can hardly push around, where if you run into another trolley people say sorry, because with a trolley so full of course you have the right of way. I like to stop to inspect the shelves and most of all I like to see if there's anything new hanging up high. This usually isn't stuff to eat; it's all those things you can never find when you look for them in the house: nail clippers, Sellotape, wrapping paper, all types of food bags, corks, bandages, plasters, tweezers, cat toys, fluorescent balls. I'd like to be able to buy all the things hanging up, just in case. Because you never know.

One time when I came to the supermarket with Mama and she brought along her last trial dad, to pretend we were a normal family, it was a real pain in the arse.

'Can I get a new crocodile pencil sharpener?'

'What do you need it for?'

Same with the paperclip holder and every other bit of stationery I want.

'What'll you do with it?'

Same with a toy mouse, one of the ones where if you wind its tail it runs round in circles.

'Blue doesn't need any fake mice. He's already enough of a mouse himself, don't you think?'

As if he didn't know that not everything that's worth having is useful.

He wasn't interested in anything beautiful, except Mama, not the towers of food wobbling in the trolleys, not the collectable family of prehistoric animals. I wonder if that guy had ever been useful for something himself, probably not, because he fell into oblivion, a deep one, along with pterodactyls and stegosauruses. One day he disappeared and no one ever mentioned him again.

I can't take a trolley now; I make do with a yellow basket. I get cat biscuits and tinned food for Blue, wafer bars and crispy pancakes for me, mini-pizzas, milk, gelato, crisps and bubble gum. I get in the queue for the people with baskets. It's a special queue, different from the one for people with trolleys – we have less stuff.

Behind me there's a man with a basket full of beer. That's all he needs, you can see it in his face. In front of me there's a girl with tomatoes and mozzarella. She's super skinny, one of those people who eat and then stick a finger down their throat so they don't get fat. Who knows what kind of pleasure she gets out of it. If you pay attention to details, if you look closely into other people's baskets, you understand all kinds of things. I realise I should have also picked up a bottle of shampoo, or detergent, something that Mama would get. Even better would be a pack of sanitary towels, because as it stands it's obvious that Mama's not around. I make up for it with some razors hanging up near the till. It's Dad who uses the razors, because I don't have a beard yet, even though I wouldn't mind having one. A beard is useless – you have one and then you have to shave it off every morning – but it's useful for dividing the men from the boys. It's a difference you wear on your face:

if you have a beard you can shop for groceries as you please; if you have a beard there's less chance people will worry whether you're an orphan or whatever.

Luckily at the supermarket everyone is busy and no one notices my basket.

When it's my turn I try to act casual. The cashier smiles at me so I smile back.

The cashier has red hair and blue make-up round her eyes that sparkles under the fluorescent lights. Her name is Daniela, I know because she has a name tag on her shirt. She knows nothing about me though and continues to smile with a bit of green leaf between her teeth.

'It comes to twenty-two fifty. Do you have that?'

'Sure I do.'

I put my things in a bag, check my change and lose myself in the crowd. I slip between the people carrying heavy bags; a moment later I'm outside.

Outside it's an afternoon like every other afternoon. Everyone seems slightly annoyed, as if they're doing things they don't want to do, as if something fun is going on somewhere else and they want the pain of grocery shopping to be over as soon as possible. They rush to fight for a parking space.

Only the Moroccans selling lighters on the

pavements seem happy to be doing what they're doing. If someone stops to buy one they rub their hands. Or maybe it's not because they're happy but because they're cold, because they had to take their hands out of their pockets. There's one who wears half-gloves, with his fingers half sticking out. He sticks out his middle finger and tells a woman wearing lots of jewellery to fuck off, then he laughs. He's got a gold tooth himself.

It's not raining any more but the cold nips the end of my nose.

Mama says that my nose looks like someone squashed a little pancake on my face. I try to lick it, but no matter how hard I try my tongue never reaches it. It's a shame. Chubby Broccolo can do it, and I always lose the bet. It would be even cooler to have a long tongue like a chameleon and to camouflage yourself like a chameleon so no one can see you. You'd become city-grey and blend in with the buildings, become asphalt-grey and turn into the pavement, become sky-grey and pray for it to do something beautiful, to open up and bring the good weather back. Opposite the supermarket is the video shop; I think about crossing the street to look in the window. They've got a cardboard cut-out of Bruce Willis stuck up on the door, but it's like Bruce is leering at me, so forget it. Who knows, maybe he really does have a sixth sense. After the video shop is the hunting and fishing shop. In the window they have real guns; you have to have a licence to buy them.

I wouldn't kill an animal again. I did it when I was little and didn't know what I was doing. I did it to lizards and even now I ask them to forgive me. Maybe everything that is happening to me is the revenge of a lizard who died for no reason, all because of a bad kid.

Then there's Intimate Secrets, an underwear store.

I wish my secret was small enough to hide under some underwear; instead I'm afraid it's so big you can see it everywhere, like it's leaking out of my coat, out of my face and eyes, out of the grocery bag, like when you step on your scarf that's slipped off without you knowing and you fall on the ground, all because of a stupid scarf.

When someone looks at me I automatically look down, like shy people do; they're always staring at the tips of their shoes. The only thing is to go on, not to look people in the face unless they look at you first, in which case smile, remember to smile.

I walk extra fast. It's better to get back as soon as possible, even if I'd rather be going back to anywhere else, to someone else's life.

Everything seems far away. Swept away by the wind and the rain.

The other side of the street is unreachable too, even if all you have to do is cross at the stripes to get to the pavement opposite.

The stripes on the street are called zebra crossings. I'd love to ride a zebra and roam through the tall grass. The lions would lick my hands like Blue when he licks up the brioche crumbs on my fingers with his rough tongue.

I hope I don't meet anyone in the lift, someone who might take a peek into my grocery bags.

Or a peek inside the flat.

9

Today is Mama's birthday.

I know, not just because I have it memorised, but also because I drew a circle with a red pen on the calendar with the famous paintings. To be honest she was the one who drew the circle, because I've never been able to reach so high, above the fridge, except with the chair.

'Don't climb on the chair because you'll fall. Don't scribble all over it because then we can't read the dates. Leave it be, I'll do it.'

On the door frame in the kitchen you can still see the notches where Mama marked how much I'd grown: two years, three years, six years . . . She always makes me stand against the same wall and act seriously, while she puckers her lips in a stern, professional way.

'Keep your head straight. If you don't keep straight, there's no point.'

But even if I try to keep straight, or stand on my tiptoes, I still can't reach above the refrigerator.

The important dates – her birthday, mine, Blue's – are all marked on the calendar with circles. It doesn't matter if things have changed; we should celebrate anyway.

I look for a birthday candle in the third drawer in the kitchen. I find ribbons from unwrapped presents, uncorked corks, unrolled rolls of string and some Chinese chopsticks that neither Mama nor I ever figured out how to use.

When we went to the Chinese restaurant the Chinese waiters all looked the same and they all watched us and laughed behind our backs, covering their mouths with their hands. We kept dropping our morsels back onto the plate or into the little bowl with the bitter black sauce that splashed everywhere, and they laughed like it was the funniest thing in the world. Mama shrugged her shoulders as if to say, 'Who cares!'

'Who cares! The Chinese always laugh; that's how they're made. Don't worry about it. Try this spling loll, it's good.'

And then lice cloquettes, flied seaweed, steamed laviolis . . . That night Mama and I only used 'L's, blinging chopsticks back to our flat with us. We blought them home to plactise in the face of the Chinese who laughed at us, even though by then I had a stomach ache, pelhaps because of having too many shlimps.

I find the little sky-blue candles from last year, sink

one into a wafer bar and light it using the lighter with the word 'Love' on it. Blue follows the whole operation intensely, mostly because the wafer wrapper sounds like the sound of dinner.

I put the wafer with the lit candle on a little saucer; it's not much of a cake but it'll do.

We make our way in procession, Blue and I, down the hallway – Blue in his grey outfit and me in my most elegant pyjamas stained with pasta sauce – single file down the hallway, careful not to trip up like always on the worn-out Persian rug that runs down the middle, which before being in our house was in Grandma's house where everyone tripped over it and swore at it too.

'Stupid rug, we've got to get rid of it one day.'

We advance as serious as can be and stop in front of the door with our special cake made of layers of wafer and vanilla cream.

I put the plate down on the ground.

The tiny candle lights the ceremony with a small, shaky glow that looks ready to go out at any moment. I'm small and shaky too. I'm not sure whether I should leave things as they are or blow for Mama, who's out of breath.

I decide to help out because the flame looks like the little lights that flicker in cemeteries and make strange shadows on the walls. Or maybe it doesn't. Maybe it's just me who finds everything gloomy.

'Happy Birthday.'

I blow and in the same breath whisper 'Happy Birthday'; even with all my practice holding my breath it feels like I don't have much air in my lungs. I leave the gift there and back up, walking backwards like shlimps do, so I can leave it there without making a sound, without anyone noticing, a little at a time.

10

On Thursday my hair grew.

You can't stop hair growing; it's one more of those 'inexorable processes' that scientists haven't yet figured out how to stop.

Hair grows at 0.00000001 miles per hour. I read it in *Strange But True*. I don't know how much a mile is but it's more than a kilometre; all those zeros make me confused. Anyway, a little bit at a time hair grows whole kilometres, even if you've got plenty of other stuff on your mind.

Usually Mama takes me to the hairdresser's before my fringe reaches my eyes. She's a hairdresser for women and I find it embarrassing to be there in the middle of all those women getting their highlights done. It's also embarrassing because the chairs are right by the window, and every so often someone passes by and sees me wearing a cape like Little Red Riding Hood next to a madwoman with a plastic cap on her head and hair coming out of the holes, while the hairdresser tugs on her goldilocks with a hooked needle.

Sometimes Frankenstein turns to me and says, 'What a beautiful child, do you like going to school?'

The word 'school' makes me think of Antonella, and I sink lower in the chair just at the thought she could pass by and see me in this get-up. As if that wasn't enough then the other women butt in, staring at me the whole time like they'd never seen a male of the species before. They're curious, they want to know everything, and they're looking for gossip, always reading magazines full of it.

I hope this torture will be over soon. I imagine that behind the jars of creams and sprays and dyes there's a magic potion that can make me disappear. Or at least make them disappear.

To be honest Mama hates going to the hairdresser's too, because then she has to make conversation, but she says it's necessary.

'One's hair should always be tidy.'

Recently she hadn't been going much herself, but I still never managed to get out of it. It's another of those strange ideas adults have: if you're older and you've got a bit of a beard already, maybe you can also wear your hair longer; if you don't have hair on your face then your hair has to be tidy, like for example the moronic cut on the head of Arseface, who in addition to having an arseface also has a dickhead's hair.

I'd rather go to a men's barber, one of the ones who have calendars with women chained up and tits as big as footballs bursting out of their black leather tops. I'd rather talk about the football match or the Grand Prix and listen to the men chatting, but Mama says she doesn't know any barbers.

'I don't want to take you to just anyone.'

If I insist she tells me to cut short the song and dance about the barbers.

Now, in theory, I could do what I want.

The problem is that at school they think about it in the same way as Mama does; they would never believe that all of a sudden she decided to let me have my way. That's why I have to cut my fringe. If I raise my eyebrows hair gets in my eyes, which is just as annoying as having a mosquito in your ear; if I pull on my fringe it hangs down almost to the end of my nose. I need to find the scissors and give myself a trim. I can't find anything better, so I try with the nail clippers. The curly strands fall into the sink like hairy parentheses. I thin things out here and there like the hairdresser does, more or less. It's a job well done, I'd say.

11

Mrs Squarzetti tells us the story of a jar that has all the evils of the world inside. If you open it they all get out.

When she passes between the rows of desks she fluffs my hair.

She's never done that before.

I'm bored. It's a sneaky kind of boredom, with an aftertaste of orange marmalade, the kind that seems sweet but then has bitter peels inside.

The box with Mama's documents, the one where she kept her secret code for the bank machine, is still on the sofa.

Sometimes Mama asks, 'Will you bring me the box with the papers?'

It's a shoebox with one side slightly crushed in, held shut with an old rubber band.

I want to open it and I don't want to open it, like in the cinema when you put your hands over your eyes at a scary bit, but then you spread your fingers to peek anyway. I found the secret code for the cash machine but I didn't search for anything else.

Now I wonder if the box might hold some other secret. I find old bills, letters from the bank, a paperclip that gets under my nail and stabs me, pages full of figures in columns but nothing to figure out, not even a reason why. Maybe that's hidden somewhere else.

Sucking my finger I wonder where.

There's a little picture of Mama copied four times in a square, one of those ones taken in a booth at the train station and then stuck onto documents. The picture didn't come out so well because it's in black and white, and because Mama's missing a piece of her head, because the stool is hard to adjust to the right height.

Davide and I also had our picture taken together last year and our heads ended up half outside the frame, in our case from the nose down.

I take it anyway and before falling asleep I put it under my pillow, next to the Madonna CD booklet. I always put something under my pillow. Usually I choose the things I'd like to dream about.

This time I put Mama times four.

12

Nearly two weeks have gone by and everything just carries on automatically.

I'm having T-shirt problems – I've run out – and all my socks are dirty and I can't change underwear every morning any more. I rotate them though, so they last longer. They're underclothes after all – no one can see if they're dirty or clean.

I should use the washing machine, but I don't know how it works. The dresser drawers look like there's been an earthquake in there, but to avoid worrying about it all I have to do is close them. My coat is full of cat hair.

The other night I even tried to smoke one of Mama's cigarettes, just to see how satisfying they really are, if it's true they soothe anxiety and make people less nervous. It was like saying, 'Fuck you, God,' nothing special, aside from the bitter taste it left in my mouth.

The house, at any rate, seems not to have noticed anything.

Except on the table in the living room: there's dust on one side and shiny wood on the other, where Blue usually lies down. If dust has been piling up for days he uses his tail like a feather duster.

As far as everything else goes there's no big difference.

Every so often I feel like crying but I don't know any more if I'm crying for me or for Mama. I cry when I think about how I can't go into her room any more like I used to when I couldn't sleep. I'd go to her and ask, 'Please can I stay in here for a while?'

And she'd say to me, 'OK, but just this once. You're a big boy now who should sleep in his own room.'

Now that I never, ever want to open her door at the end of the hallway I feel like crying. I don't know why – if it's for me who's shut out, or for her who's shut in.

I need a place to rest; I'm so tired all the time. I don't feel like doing anything, just like when I'm recovering from a cold. Sometimes I fall asleep with my head on Blue's belly. I listen to his breathing going up and down. I like hearing his heartbeat despite everything.

It's really cold in the house but the cold freezes the stink.

Blue launches sneeze attacks but it's no big deal; cats come with their very own little fur coats. I've stopped taking off my clothes. Before going to bed I take a fizzy aspirin. I hold the glass close to my ear because as the aspirin dissolves it makes the sound the sea does when the foamy waves sizzle on the rocks.

Once a day I'm frightened, because I hear the alarm clock on Mama's bedside table go off. Every day the alarm alarms me, as if I'd never heard it before. Then I remember everything. Then I slam my head down, left-right, to get rid of the thought.

When I see Antonella coming over to me during break I think I'm dreaming. It can't be true that Antonella is looking at me; she's never looked at me. When she looks towards me what she's actually doing is looking through me. Her gaze is an astral sword that stabs without wounding, as if I was transparent, made of special invisible ink that she can't read. Or doesn't want to.

And yet Antonella is coming over to me. And appears to be smiling.

'Ciao, I wanted to give you this.'

Antonella hands me an orange card, orange like the sunset on a school notebook, the sunset with palm trees on a poster for the Maldives.

'What is it?'

It's the first time just the two of us have ever talked face-to-face, alone.

It's the first time I can count the freckles on her nose, cinnamon sprinkles on whipped cream.

I say, 'What is it?'

I can't think of anything better to say.

'It's for my *Carnevale* party. You have to come in costume.'

'Oh, great, thanks.'

'Yeah, it'll be so much fun!'

Now, when you're playing a video game it can happen that you don't know what to do. There's a 50 per cent chance. Sometimes things work out, sometimes they don't. The important thing is to choose, otherwise the game can't go on. And now I can't choose. Or it's more that I have to choose not to play. No costume party, no freckle-confetti on fresh snow, no Antonella, no nothing.

'I can't come, sorry.'

'Why?'

'I'm going skiing that week.'

'Why didn't you say before?'

'I forgot about it.'

'Why don't you go skiing the week after?'

'Because the week after there'll be no more snow.'

'Wow, you should be a weatherman! How do you know?'

'What do you care?'

'I knew you were kind of an arsehole anyway. I only invited you because you're an orphan.'

There were lots of people on the beach, all happy to be on holiday, waiters carrying trays of cold drinks with little umbrellas in them, big umbrellas protecting the tourists from the sun, kids in the kid's pool, and palm trees like on the Maldives where Antonella goes on holiday, where Antonella celebrates *Carnevale*, where Antonella does what she wants. And then a wave rose up but nobody noticed: the kids kept splashing in the kid's pool, holding on to little swan or crocodile lifebelts, the mothers protected themselves from the sun, and only someone lifting a hand to his forehead, like soldiers do to peer at the enemy, started to peer at the horizon and at the sea behaving so strangely. Then the wave came and everybody died. An angry wave that wiped out everything.

All I say to Antonella is, 'I'm sorry.'

She doesn't hear me; she's already gone back to class.

I don't say anything else.

I stand there imagining the news report of disaster after disaster, all featuring me, following one after another in my head.

I keep my mouth shut until class is over for the day and I keep it shut as I walk away. I get home still silent as a mouse and enter the lobby and go up in the lift. My anger, mixed with saliva, rises from floor to floor, flaring up inside me with every beep of the floor buttons, an enormous, deafening anger, impossible to peer at from far away, a silent anger powerful enough to wipe out everything.

I lay my anger down on the sofa, beside my backpack full of undog-eared books and my blank, wordless notebook.

'Wait for me here. You too, Blue, wait just a little longer. I have to go to the bathroom.'

With my head in the toilet of my mini-adult's life, forced to wear masks every day, *Carnevale* or not, I vomit up a slimy white soul, like snot or the cum I saw squirted on some whore's tits in one of Davide's father's porno films, a stringy soul that looks like slobber, that tastes as bitter as bile and sticks to the bowl and to my chin, making snail trails that ping back and then freeze because it's so cold, streamers of pure grossness.

Hugging the toilet bowl I become big and liquid like a fucking shit.

Mama said she suffered from loneliness, that loneliness was like a whistling in her ear, like ships that set sail long ago, and she'd never reach them, not even if she swam.

Mama said that once all the ships and trains have left there's nothing left to do.

She said that's how she felt: on the shore, in the empty station, having arrived too late to life.

I can hear a whistling in my ear too.

But it's not a whistle.

It's the doorbell.

It rings and rings and won't stop ringing. Maybe somebody's stuck some chewing gum on it as a joke.

I don't know why but I get up from the toilet bowl and go to open the door.